THE CHOSEN ONE

Stephen A. Haire

Xulon Press

Copyright © 2013 by Stephen A. Haire

The Chosen One
by Stephen A. Haire

Printed in the United States of America

ISBN 9781628394375

All rights reserved solely by the author. The author guarantees all contents are original and do not infringe upon the legal rights of any other person or work. No part of this book may be reproduced in any form without the permission of the author. The views expressed in this book are not necessarily those of the publisher.

www.xulonpress.com

TABLE OF CONTENTS

Chapter 1 5
Chapter 2 11
Chapter 3 24
Chapter 4 34
Chapter 5 50
Chapter 6 64
Chapter 7 86
Chapter 8 107
Chapter 9 119
Chapter 10 133
Chapter 11 158
Chapter 12 190

Chapter 1

"Zansibar! Zansibar, where are you? Get over here, come quickly!"

"Yes, Lucarious, what do you need?" Zansibar appears from another room.

"What do I need? What do I NEED? I need a new king! That's what I need!" Lucarious shouts at him.

"What are you thinking? How could you say such a thing? You know that could get you into deep trouble with King Raaph," looking around almost ducking as if something is going to hit them.

"You mean the one who is in love with himself? The one who is greedy, who will not share his throne with another! Is that whom you are speaking about, Zansibar? Is it the same one?"

"Of course not! I am talking about King Raaph; who are you talking about?" asked Zansibar.

"I'm talking about Raaph, you fool! This one that you call king, have you ever seen him share his throne? Or allow someone to sit by his side?"

"No, Lucarious, I haven't." Zansibar still clearly does not understand. "Why do you ask me these questions? It doesn't seem like you."

"Well, let me ask you some more questions then. Am I the greatest citizen in the kingdom? Is there anyone better looking than me, Zansibar? Do I not have the most important job, and am I not the most suited to my position? Have you ever heard of me making a mistake? Can there be a single citizen who is not envious of me?"

"Yes, Lucarious, yes, you are correct," Zansibar answers.

"Well, then shouldn't he allow me just a little more? I'm not asking for much, just a little more than this... that's not too much to ask for now, is it? I mean, he is "THE KING." He has it all, anything and everything he wants. But that's clearly not enough for him, so why should it be enough for me?" Lucarious asks.

"What are you talking about? You are rambling, and none of it makes any sense. Are you feeling ok?" Zansibar asks, interrupting.

Suddenly, Lucarious grabs Zansibar by the throat and then slams him up against the wall.

"Lucarious! Huhhh Sssssstop, yooou are choking me! Please!" he gasps.

"He has everything he wants, but is it enough for him? No! No, it's not enough!" Lucarious yells. Lucarious loosens his hand and allows Zansibar to slump to the floor. Lucarious begins pacing circles around the room. "I saw the lights on in his shed."

Chapter 1

"King Raaph's shed?"

"Yes, you fool, who else has a shed? Who else would even need a shed?"

"But he hasn't used it since he created earth. That was so long ago, it feels like forever," Zansibar remarks.

"I know. So, when I saw the lights on, I went in to see what he was doing. He is in there creating again. You aren't enough for him, he is so greedy that he thinks he needs more."

"Why would he need more citizens? How many does one need?" Zansibar asks. "So, did you speak to him, then, Lucarious? Did you ask him what he was doing?"

"No. I just stood in the corner and watched. Then I left. I waited till the lights went out, and returned when I was sure that no one was around. I searched and found that he is indeed creating again, but this time it is far worse. This time he is using parts of himself to create this awful new thing."

"He didn't do that with you or me, did he?" Lucarious questions him.

"No, no he didn't," Zansibar replies.

"Then why is he doing it this time?!" asked Lucarious.

"Aren't you more than enough for him, Zansibar? Don't you give him enough worship? Clearly not, because he is going to replace you with a new creature!" Lucarious storms. "Go quickly and assemble my team. Tell them we need to practice, discuss new music, etc."

"You want to write new music? On your day off?" Zansibar asks.

"No, you fool! I need to inform my team what Raaph is working on; what he is doing and where he is taking us. We are the best he's got. Maybe we can do something to prevent any further destruction. Now go and do as I said!"

Zansibar scurries away, while Lucarious heads to the throne room.

"What are you up to, Lucarious, why are you here on your day off? It's not like you. You usually relax at home on your day off."

"Oh, I just need my baton."

"Your baton? Well, what do you need that for?"

"I decided I am going to practice."

"On your day off? You know you don't have to do that. Don't drive yourself so hard. Take the day off, relax."

"I can't, I already called the worship team to my house."

"Why, what's wrong?"

"Nothing's wrong. I just want to write a few new songs. I have some thoughts running through my head and I want to get them out before I forget what they are."

"You know, Lucarious, your team works so hard. It's ok to allow them the day off. It really won't hurt anything. And forget these new songs."

Chapter 1

"I don't want to lose them."

Belly laughing, Raaph says, "Lucarious, you are talking to me. Did you forget who I am?"

"No, of course not. Why would you say that?"

"I am the creator; not only did I create you, I gave you the desire to be worship leader. I created everything, including those songs. So if you forget them, I'm sure I can help you remember them later. You don't need to rely on yourself so much; just relax. Take the day off and work another day."

"I really feel that I need to do this. Besides, it's too late to change my mind now. I already called the worship team together."

"Okay, if you must...I guess. But don't work too hard or too long and don't drive your team too hard. You wouldn't want them to revolt on you."

"Huh? Yeah, right, revolt. Okay, sure. No revolts. Okay, well I need to go."

Lucarious starts to head for the door, but as he approaches the doorway, the door slams shut in front of him. He hears a voice from behind him.

"Oh, by the way Lucarious, are you sure there isn't something you want to tell me? Is there anything else on your mind?"

"No, why do you keep asking me? Now open the door so I can go and meet the team. They are probably all at my house by now."

"Yes, you are right. I know that they are all there waiting for you." King Raaph replies. "Lucarious you know that I love you and that I created you to be the most beautiful."

"Yes, I know that. Why are you telling me that?"

"I created you, and no one can stop you from being what I created you to be except yourself. You are the only one."

Lucarious stops and slowly looks at Raaph, then turns and again starts to walk toward the door. The door opens and he walks out.

Chapter 2

"Why are we here, doesn't he know it's our day off? Doesn't Lucarious care that we work hard all week, and when we get a day off we need that time to replenish ourselves?"

Lucarious walks into his dining room. "SILENCE! No more complaints. I've heard enough, so stop talking. I know it's your day off, but we need to talk. We have some major problems that we need to figure out."

"I thought we were practicing! Yeah, I thought we were writing new songs!" multiple voices exclaim.

"Fools, silence! Am I not in charge here, or are you?"

Everyone quickly becomes completely silent. No one has ever spoken to them that way, let alone their loving leader. "Okay, then, I thought so. Now, I brought you here today because I want you to know that I was walking around and saw the lights on in the shed."

A bunch of the team members look puzzled and glance at each other, confused.

"Why were they on? Yeah, why were they on?" They all ask each other, and then they turn back to Lucarious. A few voices echo the others' thoughts, "I thought that place was abandoned. I haven't seen the light on for years."

"It hasn't been on for years. It seems that Raaph isn't satisfied with you and me anymore. No, he needs more! We can't do enough to please him so now he wants more. More, more, more! That's all he ever wants, more! We are the best he could ever create, yet he wants something more!"

"Lucarious, be careful! We don't want to get into trouble with King Raaph," some members of the team say, looking uncomfortable.

"Trouble with mighty Raaph? TROUBLE WITH Raaph? WHAT ABOUT BEING IN TROUBLE WITH ME?!?" he screams at the top of his lungs. "What about me? I'm your leader! I'm the one who matters, no one else!"

"Uh, Lucarious, are you forgetting that he is the creator? Are you forgetting how powerful he is?"

"Of course not, I have not forgotten who he is."

"Well, he knows everything. He can read our minds. He is the creator."

"You don't know who I am! You don't know what I am capable of. You think you know me, but you don't. Just wait and see...you'll see. I am just like him. I can do things that you cannot imagine. For I am like the Creator! No, I am better than the creator! I will be just like him. I will be higher than HIM!"

Chapter 2

Everyone gasps. They can hardly believe their ears or their eyes. They all know that he just stepped over the line, and that there probably isn't any going back for him now. If he is caught saying these types of things...who knows what could happen! Nothing like this ever happened before. Who knows how the king would react?

"Lucarious, what are you doing? What are you saying, you are like him? Of course you are...we all are...we were all were created by him."

"Stopppppp...I can do things too...things that you have no idea about. Things that will blow your mind things...things...many things...things that you didn't know could be done. I will amaze you will my powers. I have powers and I can do many, many things that no one knows about. Just wait and you'll see. You'll see. Let's go. Follow me!"

"Where are we going?" they all muttered to each other.

Lucarious leads them all away from his dining room table and walks them out to his deck.

"Let's all look over to that creation he calls earth. I need to show you something." Lucarious takes them over to where they can look down at earth.

"Watch this. When I reach as far as I can, then I take my finger and place it over the ocean," and he turns it ever so slightly, "and then I just work it a little bit. It's starting, it's going and *KABOOOOOOM* there it goes! Take a look, gentlemen, at what I have done, what I started on earth. No wait... aha, see what I created on earth..."

Suddenly he starts to remember the king carrying him in his arms and how the king was always teaching him when he was a child. He taught him things—many, many things, the king hugging him and carrying him around, tickling him and telling him the secrets of everything, secrets of the universes. He remembers how King Raaph personally taught him everything Lucarious knows...showing him so many secrets....secrets that this worship team has no idea about...that no one else knows, only him. He felt so special and loved, so different from all the others.

"Lucarious, what is it? We've never seen anything like it. It's kind of fun to watch it."

"I call it a hurricane, a super storm."

"Wow, we have never heard such names. How did you come up with these names?"

The entire team is looking at each other in amazement. Not only did he create this thing, he also named it?

"Wow, this is amazing, don't you think?"

"Yeah, it's pretty amazing. I'm surprised that I didn't know."

"Booka!!"

"Yes, Lucarious?"

"Booka, you like that? Is it nice to watch?"

"Yes, Lucarious."

"And did you know I could do such things?"

Chapter 2

"No, we had no idea that you had powers, let alone great powers."

"Well, wait and see. This isn't anything. I can show you more, much more. I can show you things that are better than this. I have things that are harder than this. This is just child's play… just child's play. Not hard at all. Now watch my hurricane, it has only just begun. It's not even up to full power so let me stir it again."

They all sit back in amazement and watch. They watch as their leader creates the first storm that they are aware of. They have seen the earth from their kingdom many times but have never seen turmoil anywhere. Nothing like this is in their kingdom. How could it happen on earth?

"Now watch as I push it toward the land. See what it does to the trees and the rocks and the sand on the beach? You are about to see destruction for the first time in your life. Hahahahaha…."

"Um, Lucarious, what is destruction?"

"Destruction, you fool, is the opposite of creation. It is taking things apart. It is change…and you will become very familiar with change. Soon enough, my friend, soon enough. You are about to experience change. We are going to change things around here. The kingdom is about to look different. We will do it together. Unlike the king. He does it by himself. He does everything by himself. We are different from him…we help each other, we work together and we will be together."

The Chosen One

They all continue to look down to earth and watch his new thing that they have never seen. They can't look away, although part of them feels like they should. They just want to see what happens. They need to see what happens. This is the most exciting thing they have seen in a long time, so amazing, so awesome to watch.

"Have you ever seen something so powerful? See how it whips the trees around and it tosses the leaves like they are nothing. It bends them and rips the leaves off all the trees."

"Is that ok, Lucarious? Isn't that a little too much? I mean, it's getting close to the king's pets."

"His pets? His pets! You are concerned with his pets?!? He isn't concerned with his pets, so why should you be concerned with them?"

"Lucarious, why do you say he isn't concerned with them?"

"Because he is not concerned…just look at them! All these ugly creatures, they just walk around and eat the grass and the leaves. They are boring and UGLY. But typical King Raaph, he couldn't just have a pet! He had to create a place for them to live and even that was not good enough …no, no it wasn't… was it enough? Of course not! Well, what did he do next? He created a star to keep them warm and he, he even gave them a night light…aah, isn't that cute? A little light so they could see in the dark. Wouldn't want them to fall into the ocean now, would we? Dumb stupid ugly creatures with no purpose. I asked

Chapter 2

him once, 'What is their purpose?' and do you know what he said to me? Do you? Do you know what he said?!?"

"No, Lucarious, of course not."

"He said, 'Because when I thought of them, they put a smile on my face.' So he had a thought and then he created a zoo. A place just for them to live. He just watches them from here; he never goes and visits them. He made them a star to keep them warm but that wasn't enough. Oh no, good ole king, he had to go out and create other planets around them just to hold his zoo in place. He is so over the top, everything has to be extravagant. Can't just have a pet, no, has to build them their own universe! Ridiculous! Completely over the top as usual...."

"Um, Lucarious, don't you think you should stop the storm? It's getting close to his pets."

"Why should I care about his pets? If he cared so much as he says he does, then how come they are aging; why are they turning old? I've even seen some that were so old, they fell asleep and never woke up."

"Well, you better hurry."

Lucarious sighs a huge sigh. "Why must I do everything?" He reaches down and lets the storm head towards his hand. He allows it to go into his hand and he pulls his arm back from over the balcony and then takes his other hand and shakes them together. And boom, it's gone. This makes his friends even more amazed.

"It didn't hurt him and it stopped right away. That storm was huge and he put it out with just his bare hands. He must have more power than we have given him credit for."

"You think that was amazing? I have more lots more."

"Show us Lucarious, show us!"

"Ok, one more, then that's it."

Lucarious tells them for this one they will have to go to the earth, so the team all heads down. They go as fast as they possibly can.

As they are on their way, Lucarious yells, "Quickly! We must move quickly and get back before anyone notices we are gone."

They all land at the foot of what seems to be a mountain.

Lucarious says, "Watch and see. I will create smoke from out of a mountain. I will make smoke and fire come out of the top of this mountain."

They all look at each other and think to themselves, "He has finally lost it." So Lucarious jumps up as high as he can and with the greatest force possible, he lands on the side of the mountain. With the pressure of the force, smoke comes flying out of the top of what they think is a mountain. He laughs and laughs and laughs. They all stand still with their eyes almost bulging out of their heads. They are amazed at what just happened. They can hardly believe it happened, let alone that Lucarious made it happen. Lucarious jumps up even higher and with all that is in him, he

Chapter 2

lands harder than ever. He forces himself against the mountain. *Kaboom*! Out of the top flies even more smoke and red liquid. The liquid pours out the top and it slides down the side of the mountain. Before the liquid touches the trees, the trees catch on fire and burn up; this makes this entire situation even more amazing. No one can believe their eyes.

"Now that, my friends, is something powerful. That is something worth watching. I told you I could create things. Now hurry and let's get back before we are noticed."

"Uhhh, Lucarious, what about that red liquid stuff, what are you going to do about that?"

"Well my friends, it will soon stop on its own. It will be fine. Now let's go."

They quickly leave and go straight back to Lucarious' house. Lucarious starts with a new speech.

"Remember a few things. First, I personally hand-picked all of you. It was my idea, my will, and my decision who was and was not a part of the worship team. I picked the instrument, I taught you how to play, and I taught you how to be on time. In fact I taught you what musical timing is. It is my creation. So now you know I am like Him. I created you and your destiny; I created the music and light show. Now from nothing, I created a storm on the earth and fire from a mountain. Do I need to keep showing you that I am able to create? The king is not the only one who creates around here."

"Secondly, think about how much King Raaph loves his worship. Oh, how he loves to be worshiped. That gives us the upper hand. Not to mention I can do so many more things that you don't even know about. We need to get ready and we need to go and we need to have me sit on the throne beside him. We need me to be just like him. We need the rest of this kingdom to worship me so that I can promote you. Imagine, you will be even more loved than you already are. The citizens of this kingdom will love respect and admire you! You will also be able to be in charge of your own area. I will promote you. I will make you strong. I will make you famous. I will give you everything you need. I will give you everything you want. I won't hold back on anything from you. Every citizen will look at you the way they look at me. Not only that.... hahaha, I'm going to give you each your own day to sit on the throne to rule and reign the entire kingdom for an entire day. I will do it! I willllllll! Hahahahahahha..."

"Lucarious?"

"Yes, Landalin, what is it?"

"Lucarious, what if he...he says no, what if he gets mad?"

"Don't you worry Landalin; I have a plan if he does. Start to get ready. I don't know what will come. I will start to hint around to him and we will see where it takes us. We can never forget; we can never under estimate how important we are. We are the worship team. He needs us...he loves to be

Chapter 2

worshiped so much...what would he do without us? Huh? What, what would he do? I can tell you that without us, he would not have any worship music ... could you imagine his kingdom in total silence? He'd never have it that way. He'd never have it. No way could he stand it silent, look at it now—we all work in shifts...just to keep him going."

"I don't know, Lucarious. I just don't know. It might not work, it might backfire, I'm sure he already knows what we are talking about. I mean remember when I wrote that new song for you?"

"Yes, I remember, why? Why do you bring that up now?"

"Because as we were walking in the throne room before we even open our cases he looked right at me and called my name. I said, "Yes, King, what is it?' He told me, 'I really like your new song.' We hadn't even played it yet! He had that look in his eye like, 'I gave it to you, I put it in your mind' type of look.

"Neesha, did you tell him you wrote the song? Did you?"

"Yes, Lucarious, I told him I wrote it. I mean what was I going to say, I mean really?"

"You could have told him the truth and say that we wrote it together and not taken all the credit...are you trying to take my job, Neesha, are you...?"

"No, of course not. Why are saying that? Why are you so mad? I don't understand."

"I'm mad because I told him we wrote it, you ungrateful...haaaaaa... never mind. It's too late.

Things will be different. Now go and rest. Be ready for another meeting in the future. I don't know when, but be ready all the time so that when I do call you together you will be here fast. If he doesn't share it, then we will meet again to figure out how to make him share it with us. Go home now."

Lucarious leaves his house leaving every one behind.

They start asking Zansibar questions. "Zansibar, are you now in charge?"

"I guess so. Why do you ask?"

"Because we have questions."

"Like what kind of questions?"

"Like what happened to Lucarious?"

"What kind of question is that? How do you expect me to answer that?"

"Well before today he was King Raaph's favorite. He and King Raaph had such an amazing relationship. Why is he acting this way, why is he mad?"

"Well, ummm, he, well he...ok, but I didn't tell you this. He asked the king if he could sit on the throne and be worshiped. He wanted to sit there and have the worship team go on without him. He wanted; well he wanted to have the king's honor and admiration."

"Well, go on, tells us more."

"What happened, it's like this. The king laughed because he thought that Lucarious was teasing him, joking around. Lucarious told him he wasn't joking and said, 'Stop laughing, I am serious.' Then King Raaph told him that he would never be able to share

Chapter 2

his throne with another; that he would just have to be satisfied with the position that he already gave to Lucarious. Lucarious said to the king, 'You should share it with me. It won't hurt a thing to allow me to be worshiped along with you…to see what it is like is all I ask, that's not much.' Then King Raaph told him that he was the only one who would be worshiped and he was the only one that would sit upon the throne. Lucarious had the guts to ask him why he was acting this way! Can you believe it? Wow, if I didn't see him mad myself I wouldn't have believed it."

"But, go on."

"Ok, then the king said to him. 'Nothing I created will share my throne. Nothing created will share in my wisdom and knowledge and nothing created can be worshiped …ever! It just can't happen.'

"So, then what?"

"Well Lucarious stared at him for a minute and then he walked away. You could tell that he was not happy at all."

"When did all of this happen?"

"Just a few days ago and he hasn't stopped obsessing over it since. I keep taking him to some of his favorite places to be, but nothing is changing him. I am concerned about him. He is obsessed. He won't stop thinking about it or think about anything else for that matter."

Chapter 3

Lucarious then walks toward the shed that is behind the palace. He sees the lights are on, so he leaves to come back later, but notices that the lights are turning off. He hides and waits for awhile then goes into the shed that Raaph calls his lab. It has beakers full of blue colors with smoke rolling off the top of them. Some are boiling and others are percolating. He walks around looking for information. There it is, the clip board, the famous clip board. He immediately remembers the time when King Raaph had all the names of the citizens of the kingdom listed on it. He sat down and allowed Lucarious to hand pick the names of all the worship team, young Lucarious wanted to give everyone a job. He wanted everyone to play an instrument. Raaph wanted so much to give him everything he wanted but he knew that it was not possible. He said, "I'll tell you what, I will give you up to one third."

"Oh come on King, give me half. I need half and they will love their job, they will be so happy and I will be their friend and leader. We will all

Chapter 3

work together forever and you will have awesome music forever."

King Raaph smiled at him and messed up his hair a little bit. He thought about it and said, "Sorry, that's not the plans I have for you. I'd love to give you half but I need messenger and warrior citizens. So I will give you up to one third."

THUD. Lucarious snapped out of his daydream, he then realizes that he was day dreaming. He'd better hurry; he had no explanation on why he was where he was. If the king saw him in the shed he would have to come up with a reason on why he was hanging out where he had no reason to be. So quickly he reviewed the charts and the information. When he came to the last page, his face turned red and he dropped the clip board. He just read something that would change him forever.

He read that the king was actually using some of his own life force, some of his own life cells and life fluid to make this next creation. The creation destination was earth. He started to remember another time when he was very young and playing ball with the king. He asked why he wasn't just like his king. "I mean, you are my father, why don't I look like you? Why don't I have everything that you have? I want to be you, king. Can't I be your son?"

"Haha little one, someday you will be a great one in my kingdom. You will be in charge of a lot and you will love it. You don't need to be just like me. You don't need to be created in my image. Your image is just fine, it's perfect! I like the way I created you."

"Please king, pretty please? Can you just change me just a little bit? Please…….?"

"Go on little one and put away your toys, it will soon be time for the great feast."

As he caught himself daydreaming, he realized he was already there too long. He'd better hurry. He takes one long last look and shakes his head. "Made in his image with his life cells, his own body parts, I can hardly believe it. What is he doing? What is he doing?!? He is unbelievable! He just can't get enough of himself. He is so outrageous. I can't stand to think about him anymore. Who would be so greedy that he wouldn't share with me? He told me I could have whatever I wanted, I would be in charge and all I am asking for is to sit beside him and to see what it is like to be worshiped. How hard is that? How could it even affect him? How would he even notice? It couldn't possibly hurt. I think I will try it. I think I will sit on his throne the next time he is not in the throne room. Doesn't he realize how important I am to the kingdom? Could you imagine what it would be like? I don't think I even remember silence in the kingdom. I'm sure if we stood up and were quiet, he would only be able to stand it for awhile and then he would give up and he would give me what I want."

Then suddenly he caught a whiff of something strange, a terrible, awful smell. He looked and saw that it was coming from a barrel in the corner. He

Chapter 3

walked forward to see and heard a noise coming from behind the shed. He froze for what seemed forever. When no more noises came, he slowly crept toward the windows. He looked out all the windows and saw nothing so he snuck out the door.

"I'll be back, I must find out what he is up to. He's got something strange going on here. What was that smell? It was gross, whatever it was. I will have to figure it out when I have time. I need to wait till he leaves again so I can be sure he won't be back so I can look around."

Lucarious heads home to rest. He has work to do tomorrow.

Lucarious decides to go into the throne room early as usual. He doesn't want anything to seem out of the ordinary.

"Good morning, King Raaph."

"Good morning, Lucarious, did you rest well?"

"Yes, my king, I did rest very well."

"Good, good, good, I'm so glad to hear that. I hope you didn't work your team too hard."

"What?" Lucarious looks at him puzzled.

Raaph says, "Yesterday when you and your team were writing new songs. I hope you didn't work them too hard."

"Oh, oh no, I didn't. I forgot what you were talking about. But yes, thanks, we had a great time yesterday. We mostly sat around and talked."

"Well I'm glad to hear that. You and your team need to spend time together, not just here on the stage but also during your off hours. They look up to you and think highly of you, Lucarious."

"Oh, really? I guess so, I never thought about it much."

He is nervously picking up instruments and checking them for being in tune. "No, I guess I never thought about it; but I guess you're right. I guess you know them better than I do, my king."

"Well treat them right and don't lead them astray. They love you. Must I remind you how big a responsibility that is?"

"I ... I ... I ... don't think you need to. I know my responsibilities."

"Just remember, loving your team is one of the many responsibilities that I entrust you with."

"I know, I know, don't worry, they are fine."

"Ok, Lucarious, I just don't want you to forget."

"Well, I should get the team in here; it's about time we start."

"Wait, Lucarious."

"What is it my king?"

"Have you been down to the earth?"

"To earth? Why? Why would you ask me that question?"

"Well as I looked down at it last night before bed, I realized there were trees that had huge amounts of leaves missing."

"Leaves missing, huh? That is strange, wonder why?" As he says this, he feels that sickening feeling in his stomach like he knows he's about to get caught.

Chapter 3

"Ok, if you don't know anything, then I'm sure no one else would."

"King, don't you think that you should go and check it out. I mean aren't those leaves the life force that you made for those pets of yours?"

"Yes, it is, why do you ask?"

"Well maybe you better go and check on them, maybe something strange has happened and they are eating all the leaves off of one area. Maybe you should go and check, look around and see what is going on. You wouldn't want your pets to be in trouble and you didn't save them. You wouldn't want them hurting if it wasn't necessary."

"Well, Lucarious, you should know by now that even when one of my pets sheds its older skin off, I know about it. In fact I even know how much skin they shed and how much it weighs."

Lucarious' lump in his throat seems to be growing bigger by the second.

"I see," he says. "Ok, then, you know what you are doing, never mind."

"No, I think you are right. I think that I need to go down and look around. It has been a long time since I was down there."

"I'm sure they would love to see you my king."

"Yes, and I would love to spend time with them and speak to them, every one of them, make sure they know I haven't forgotten them."

"Yes, that sounds like a nice visit. Probably long overdue, huh, king?"

"Yes, Lucarious it's long overdue."

That afternoon when the worship team stopped and went home to eat their lunch, the king also returned back home. Raaph enters in and shuts the door. He stands there in silence for a moment and listens. He thinks he hears a noise upstairs so he runs up the steps. As he quickly walks down the hall he pokes his head in the many rooms. He finally sees her.

"Kadesha, there you are. I have wonderful news, I decided to take a break and go and visit the zoo. I need a vacation and they need to see me."

"That's wonderful Raaph. I'm sure they will be pleased to see their master."

"Yes, yes, that's what I thought; the citizens could use a break."

"They could have themselves some time to work on their houses," Kadesha interrupts him, "Or they could just relax and take a break. Yes, yes, you are right, you are always right. No need for them to work so hard. They could use a vacation too, you know."

"Yes, of course. I'm just excited to see my pets, it's so much different walking and spending time with them, than watching from a distance. It should be fun. I agree. I'm going to pack my suitcases."

Ding dong.

Lucarious looks and wonders who is at his door. Eeeerrreeek. The door opens and standing at his door is a messenger citizen. In fact, it's the leader, Nemola.

"Yes, Nemola, come in, come in. It's been a long time since you were here."

Chapter 3

"Thanks, Lucarious." Nemola looks around and sees everything to be pretty much normal. Everything looks the same as the last time he was there.

"What can I do for you?"

"Well, Lucarious, King Raaph asked me to come and get you."

Lucarious eyes widen and he gets a knot in his throat. "Really he...he wants to talk to meee? I wonder why, do you know what is about?"

"Oh yes, Lucarious, he wants you, me, and Kanamoola in the ruling chambers."

"Really? Why would he call the three leaders together? Is there a problem?" Lucarious holds his breath after each sentence; he stares at his visitor without blinking.

"No, no problem, he just wants to tell us what we should be doing and watching for as he leaves for a vacation."

"Puhhhh," Lucarious lets out the air and lets his shoulders drop just a little. "Oh, oh, ok."

"Lucarious is there something wrong?"

"No, why do you ask?"

"You seem...um...uptight. Are you ok?"

"Yes, yes of course. I'm fine. I just was confused. It's been so long since you visited me and even longer since Raaph held a meeting with us three. Probably even longer since Raaph took a vacation. Yes, shaking his head, I agree it's been a longtime, a well deserved vacation, I'm sure of that. It can't be easy being King Raaph. He has to care for all of the citizens; he has to make sure there is enough food and water, and consider all of the things he created. That can't be easy I'm sure. Yeah, you're right Nemola, and it's only going to be harder."

"Harder, Lucarious, why would you say that?"

"Because of the new creation. It can only make him more work."

"New creation? Whatever are you talking about?"

"Oh, oh, uh, well uh, you see, um, well."

"Oh, never mind, I forgot whom I am talking to, of course you know something that no one else knows."

"Huh?"

"You know, Lucarious, you aren't fooling me."

"I'm not?"

"Of course not. Everyone knows that King Raaph and you are best friends. I mean, really, you are the only citizen who could ever be bold enough to not add the King part when you are talking about King Raaph."

"Hahaha." Lucarious stops for a minute being caught off guard, and says to himself, "You know, I never noticed I was the only one who didn't add the King part to his name."

"That's interesting, huh, King Raaph actually seems ok that you don't address him as King."

"Really, I never thought about it."

"You never thought about it? Come on, are you kidding me? Everyone wants to be you; everyone wants the king to be his best friend. It must be nice.

Chapter 3

But don't worry, Lucarious, I won't tell anyone nor will I let on that I know anything. You can trust me."

"Thanks Nemola. Raaph would be mad if I told you his secrets. I almost let it slip. Please remember, no one."

"Don't worry, Lucarious, I wouldn't do that to you. Now come on he is waiting. We shouldn't keep him waiting."

"Yes, you are right, let's not keep KING RAAPH waiting."

" Hahahahaha… that's funny Lucarious, you just called him King, hahahaha, it must be nice to be you."

"If you only knew my friend, if you only knew."

Chapter 4

They leave the house and head toward the throne room. It doesn't take long since Lucarious's house is the closest house to the king's home. When they enter, Kanamoola is already there standing in silence, just waiting. When Kanamoola is standing he is extremely intimidating. It's no wonder that King Raaph made him ruler of the warrior citizens. Just looking at him was enough to keep any of the citizens in line. Lucarious suddenly remembered when King Raaph was training Kanamoola. Lucarious would watch them for hours. Sometimes he would have been warned and sent back to his room to practice. Lucarious knew Raaph loved him and wouldn't hurt him so he would sneak back out to the balcony and watch for hours. Raaph would push Kanamoola and push and push. Lucarious would get upset when he thought that Raaph was too hard on him. He thought that he should let him have fun. But later it all made sense when everyone started to notice that Kanamoola's arms were growing and his stomach was hard as a rock. Everyone also noticed that he

Chapter 4

was quiet and patient. He could stare straight ahead for hours while they teased him. Poor Kanamoola, they thought, he isn't allowed to move, no matter what we do to him.

But now many years later, it all made sense. He was a mighty warrior citizen, the mightiest and then most self disciplined warrior in the kingdom.

It was so much fun growing up together in the king's castle, everyone had their own room and they would sneak into each other's room and talk late into the night until they fell asleep. They would laugh and giggle so hard, they didn't know how the king didn't wake up and hear them. Looking back, he probably did. They would wonder why the king would be so loving one minute, but then so demanding that they become who he wanted them to be. THE DESTINY walk, the king called it. They would try to make voices that sounded older and more mature. They tried to sound just like their father the king.

"Kana, walk the destiny walk," "Nem, walk your destiny." Peeeehhahaha! They would all fall off the bed giggling at the voices Lucarious made.

"Lucarious, Lucarious, Lucarious, what, huh, oh."

"Yes, what is it?"

"Lucarious, I asked you if you were listening to me."

"No, uh, sorry, I wasn't paying attention. What did you say?"

"I said that I am leaving and that I am going on a vacation. A long overdue vacation, I might add. Yes, Lucarious, you are correct I need to do this more often. It's been awhile since I spent any time with my pets so I am going to earth and I am going to spend time with them and thoroughly enjoy time with each one of them."

"Good, you deserve it. Have fun and take your time. Don't worry about us, we will watch over the kingdom for you. There will be no problems or anything for you to worry about."

"Lucarious, I am not worried. There will be no worries in the kingdom."

"Oh, uh, sorry. Don't concern yourself with us up here. You go down to the earth and have a great trip and take your time."

"Lucarious, I hope you're not trying to get rid of me."

"Get rid of you? Why of course not, why would you think that? Hahahaha, I'm just teasing you."

"I'm glad that you are excited for me and my vacation. Oh, and while I'm gone, take some time and surprise me with some new songs. You know how much I love new songs."

"Yes, Raaph I do know how much you love your music. Believe me, I know."

"Well, ok, then I am leaving all three of you in charge. All the citizens will be informed of my departure and will be informed that I am entrusting you three to take care of everything."

"Oh, don't even think about us Raaph, just have fun. We will rule your kingdom for you and it will be perfect when you return."

Chapter 4

"Lucarious, no need to rule anything. There is just one ruler in this kingdom and it is me. You are just my leaders; that is all. So don't try to rule over the citizens as that might confuse them or even upset them. I wouldn't want to come back early."

"Oh, no, please take your time, don't come back early! There won't be any need for it. No problems, no ruling, huh guys, we wouldn't be ruling, will we?"

"No, Lucarious, we won't be ruling, we will just be watching. Watching over everything for our king."

The obsitorium was especially built to look down to earth. It is an easy way to see the part of the earth that is facing you. The deck was also built to look at the earth. But if you want to see what is going on when it is night time on the earth, you must go into the obsitorium and look there in the mirror scope. This mirror scope uses the moon to reflect the dark side of the earth. Since earth was only created with one body of land, if the king wanted to see his pets at night he must use it. King Raaph then picks up his bags and walks on the deck and then to the lookout ledge at the obsitorium.

He smiles and says in a shouting voice, "I'll be back in a little while."

He jumps of the cliff, keeping his feet and body in perfect stance so when he lands on the earth, he will land gracefully.

With the king out of the way, nothing can stop him. No one would ever venture into the shed. He has all the time he needs. He can take his time and really explore. He can do whatever he pleases. The entire messenger team has already had the entire kingdom assembled in one place to see off their beloved king. The one they love and the one they know loves them.

So Lucarious turns to them and speaks to all the of the kingdom citizens. He says, "Fellow citizens, and especially my praise and worship team. The king has left the kingdom so now we have been all granted a vacation. There is no reason for us to be performing, as we are all on a vacation while Raaph is on vacation. My team will practice while he gone. I will let you know when it is time. So go and have some fun. You are dismissed."

The citizens turn and head toward their homes.

He heads back to the shed. "I must find out what that smell was. I just can't get it out of my head. I never smelled anything like it." What possibly could be the reason for something that terrible. Lucarious was used to everything in the kingdom smelling so beautiful.

"What possible reason could he have for making such a thing? I can't possibly think of any."

He quietly opens the door just enough to slip in. This time he was sure no one would be around for a long time. As he was looking around he thought to himself, "How could I stay in here and watch him work? I wish I could stand here and see what he is up to without him seeing me. I need to somehow watch him while he is in here. Hummm, how could I do it, I need to figure that out but it will have to wait for

Chapter 4

later. Ok, now where was that big drum with that putrid smell? It was in the corner the last time I was here but it's not here. I wonder where it went. I know it's here, I can still smell that smell. I'm not sure I'll ever forget what smell. What reason would he have with making something that wasn't pleasing? I just don't understand; everything in his kingdom was so pleasing."

So he continues to search for it to see where it was moved to. He realizes that there are other rooms inside the shed. He never realized how big this place was. He really hadn't been there since he was very young and very little. Back then it seemed huge but he only remembered one room.

"Well I guess all of these rooms were here, I just didn't realize it, nor did I go into the other rooms."

So he slowly heads into the other room. After entering the room, he sees the room is filled with charts and graphs hanging on the walls. There is a huge book. "No one could possibly ever miss that book," he thinks to himself. It has numbers then a name and another number then a name. Name after name after name. It seems to go on forever. He then flips to the last page and it is filled with names.

"That's strange," he thought to himself. So he flips around inside the book and he sees there are names and after these names there are some blanks. He moves his finger to the top of the page where it is blank. It says place of birth, destiny walk, gifts, choice made and final destination.

"Why is this blank and what does this all mean? Where could their destination be? His pets that fall asleep and never wake up don't have a destination. They are just gone forever. He sure is doing something strange here. He sure is putting a lot of effort into this new project. I wonder if it was like this before he created the citizens that live here with him now. Hummm, very interesting."

"Well, I'll come back later. What it behind this door?"

He heads into the next room. There are drawings and sketches of weird creatures.

"These guys are just as ugly as, if not uglier than the pets he already has. Is he also making more pets?" As he looks at them, he compares their size to the trees. He realizes that the trees seem huge compared to these new pets.

"What are these for, he already has a zoo and the piece of land on the earth is full of creatures. Where is he going to put these new creatures? There isn't any room for them now. I don't understand his thinking. Could he be planning on another earth? Is that possible? He told me that the universe that he created around the earth is perfect. That nothing can be added or taken away from it or it wouldn't work correctly. That is one thing he is so proud of. Although he has made millions of universes with nothing in them, I thought that they would stay empty and they were just a waste. A waste, as usual just a waste, just a show of extravagance. Him and

Chapter 4

his extravagance. Nothing can be plain and simple, everything must be over the top. Over the top life for an over the top king. What arrogance. So what else is here, what could be sitting around here? So many rooms, so many clues. Why did I never realize these rooms existed before?"

He then remembers that these rooms couldn't have been here. "They weren't there before, they are all new. They have to be new." He used to play hide and seek in here and there was only one room and one door. "When did he add these rooms and how did no one else notice them before? How did no one else ever know that he was adding on? The citizens should have at least heard some noises, wouldn't you think or at least they should have seen him adding on. Did he do it himself; I've never seen him work like this before? You would think that if he had someone adding on that someone would have talked about it. I don't get it, I'm so confused. Ahhhh, who really cares? I just need to find out why he is doing it."

As he heads towards another door all he can do is shake his head in amazement. He opens the door and then suddenly he just about falls to the ground with an overwhelming smell. That terrible, terrible smell. It was so overwhelming that he jerks his head to the left and backwards so much that he ends up taking two steps backwards. He sighs a long sigh.

"Oh, wow, that's terrible."

He shakes his head and blinks his eyes a couple of times. He takes a deep breath and enters the room. He walks in just far enough for the door to close behind him. He stands very still, using just his eyes to scan the room, as he is still holding his breath. He steps towards a work bench in the middle of the room. He looks down at the files laying there. And puuuuuuh. He can't hold his breath any longer. He realizes it's no use, so he just accepts the horrid smell into his nostrils. He reaches down and picks up the files and notices every one of them has a red stamp that says TOP SECRET.

"What is this?" he says out loud as he is jingling a small lock on the file.

"Ok, this is getting very weird. Why would he lock this file and what's inside? What is he hiding, what could possibly be so important that he would lock it up? He is getting even weirder by each room."

The only other thing in the room that is worth looking at is the 55 gallon drum with that smell coming out of it like a fog. He reaches down and grabs the lid and looks into it. Even more fog comes rolling out of it and it seems to be a liquid inside. The smell is coming from the liquid. It appears to be light brown liquid and on the edges of the top of the drum there is a yellow powdery substance. As he looks away because the smell is so over powering, he notices a shelf with glass cups and tubes all over it.

Each tube has written words he is unfamiliar with. First one is acid, next says sulfur, and on and on they go. Just below that shelf, there are some weird

Chapter 4

looking metal handles that remind him of spoons or maybe forks.

"But the bottom is missing. And why are there wooden spoons? I have never seen spoons made from wood. I mean really, that is weird; wood is mostly used for trim, tables and chairs. A wooden spoon? How strange." Then notices a new metal spoon and he wants to look closer at the liquid so he dips it in to the drum. More smoke and fog come rolling out. So he quickly pulls it out and now it's a rod just like the others.

He thinks to himself, "What is this stuff, it melted the spoon?"

So he lays it beside the other ones. He can hardly stand the smell which only increased when he dipped the spoon into the liquid, he looks around and decides it time to leave. He turns and heads for the door and jumps backwards, tripping over himself and falling to the ground, never allowing his eyes to move from whatever is staring at him. He thought he was alone; his heart is pounding right through his chest. Everything is going in slow motion.

"I thought I was alone, I didn't know anyone was here, how am I going to explain myself? How could I be here and not be in trouble, how could I not have seen him?"

He freezes and doesn't move from the position that he fell to, motionless, just staring at the eyes of this thing that was watching him. It doesn't move so he says, "You scared me." They still don't move. He stands to his feet and loudly says, "Why won't you answer me? Still nothing, so he walks over to it. He reaches out to touch it and still nothing, so he grabs it and it is not a citizen. In fact it's a suit of some kind, almost like clothes. It has a zipper down the front and a hat that you put over your head and face. He puts the hat on and looks out through what he thought was the eyes. He takes a normal breath and realizes that the smell is gone. Although his breathing is making a funny loud noise, the smell is all gone.

"So this is how he stands to be in this room. It cancels all the rotten smell. Very interesting, very interesting. I'll have to use this next time I come."

He places it back exactly as he found it, pushing it around and adjusting it till it is just…so. He walks out through the swinging doors and sighs and takes a long deep breath. He looks all around as he makes sure no one saw him. He turns around and looks through the doors and windows.

"I wonder what could possibly be in those files. Why would he lock them up; what could be such a secret? I don't like how he is becoming so secretive. I will find out what is in there."

Lucarious heads home and lies down on his bed. As he lies there, he tries to figure out how he can see what King Raaph is doing in the labs.

"I must find out what he is doing. I can't stand it any longer, there is something going on, but if I don't watch him how can I know what he is really up to? There are many questions that need answers,

Chapter 4

many questions that need to be addressed. There is something going on that just doesn't feel right to me. I'm sure if I go in with him he will show me some, but will he tell me what is in the top secret folders? Raaph thinks that everything is fine and everything is perfect. Well it just isn't so. But he doesn't know that, so maybe I can get him to show me. That is what I will do. I don't have anyone that I could place in there to watch him, no one small enough that he wouldn't see them watching him. That wouldn't work out very well...what can I do? Hum. What about the thing that he used to use when we were growing up so that we could remember what we looked like when we were very small? If I placed those machines, then I could see him working and if they took enough pictures maybe I could piece the puzzle together along with the information that he tells me. Then I will know everything. I can use that to my advantage. That is an important key to this operation. I am sure there must be cameras in that one room or maybe in another room. I should go and look around, maybe I can find cameras small enough he wouldn't notice them in there. I will have to go to the palace tomorrow."

The next morning Lucarious goes into the castle and walks around the throne room. He picks up instruments and plucks them, adjusting the tuning knobs, checking the straightness of the necks on some of them. He is sure that no one is near or looking around, he heads to the back and opens the door leading down the hall. He doesn't see anyone, so he goes back and grabs another instrument and tunes it, while peering down the hall. There still isn't any movement. No one seems anywhere near the palace. He gently places the instrument in its holder and sneaks down the hall looking all around and behind his shoulder. He quickly finds the room he is looking for; he stops and takes notices of hundreds of pictures stuck to the walls. There is no rhyme or reason why they are placed where they are, no time line. They are just stuck to the wall. They aren't even straight. As he notices pictures of his childhood, he remembers…he and the king swinging around and around. The king would love to play games where he would swing and swing and swing you and then let go only to have another citizen fly to catch you before you hit the ground. It was a lot of fun. It was exciting as you always wondered if you were going to hit the ground. The citizens that were catching didn't help the matter. They too, loved to wait until the very last second to catch you and cushion your fall.

    He realizes he is day dreaming again. "I better hurry and find the room."

    He heads into a room and starts to look around. "I think this is the room," he says to himself.

    "Haahum, what are you doing Lucarious?"

    "Oh, you scared me."

    "Woh, a little jumpy are we Lucarious?

    "I didn't see you."

Chapter 4

"What are you doing Lucarious, why are you here and why are you alone? You know the king isn't here, you know he left."

"Yeah, I know."

"So why are you walking around inside the palace unattended without the king being here? You know you shouldn't be sneaking around."

"Sneaking around? Who says I am sneaking around?"

"Well then what are you doing, why are you here?"

"I came for memories. I wanted to see the pictures and I wondered why Raaph hasn't taken any pictures lately. I wanted to see the camera. I was considering taking some pictures."

"Why would you need to do that?"

"Well I thought it would be nice to...uh...have some... uh...pictures like we used to take."

"Why, Lucarious, would you ever need pictures?"

"Uh, well...uh...I thought I needed to take some so we could remember what we look like, things like that."

"Lucarious, you know as well as I do that the season of aging is over and that everyone will now look the same for eternity. That is why he put away the camera and doesn't use it anymore."

"Oh, I didn't know that is why he quit using it."

"There is no need for it; it can stay in the drawer forever. Now you should get moving and leave before you get yourself into trouble. There is nothing in here for you Lucarious."

"Ok, I'll head back to the house and do some work there, wouldn't want to upset Raaph."

"Lucarious, why is it that you are the only citizen that doesn't address my husband as King? Every other citizen has enough respect that they always call him King Raaph, but not you. Why is that, why do you choose to be less respectful of your King?"

"Uh, um, I never thought about it."

"Lucarious, do you really expect me to believe that you, his best friend, the one he spends the most time with of all citizens, you didn't realize that you were being dishonoring to the King? Must I remind you that you were the one that he chose? You need to be the best of the best. You need to be the most respectful and the most humble and the most loving and caring in the entire kingdom. Everyone knows that you are the one who is chosen and that you are the favored one and that you are the loved one. Please think before you speak and think before you act, you seem to be a little reckless lately and need to reexamine your heart. It is time to reexamine your heart. Why, you know in your heart you should be a better role model, now go and think about working on yourself and changing your attitude."

"Kadesha, you have nothing to worry about. The king has never corrected me and told me to add the "King" part to his name."

"Lucarious I can't believe that you are talking to me this way. What is wrong with you? Of course he won't correct you; he loves you and honors you and

Chapter 4

what you do. He wants you to be bright enough to figure things out on your own. You are supposed to learn that he didn't create robots nor does he want to be a baby sitter. I suggest that you start working on the inside of yourself before the inside of you destroys who you were created to be. Trust me, there is nothing better than whom you were created to be and if you choose differently, you will only choose less of a life than what the king has for you."

CHAPTER 5

After a few days the king returns from his vacation. He decides to go back to work. As King Raaph walks into the room, the doors swing shut and the overwhelming stench from the drum doesn't even phase him. Instead of reaching for his gas mask he stands there frozen just staring at the huge book sitting on the work bench. He begins thinking about what is in there, whose names are listed in there. How he never intended for it to be this way; it was supposed to be all about love, one hundred percent pure love. Consequences for poor choices was never the thought, never the intention. It shouldn't have to be this way. Should he end it all now before he had even begun?

He walks out of the room and back to his house. Once he gets inside his house, he sits down and stares at the wall. His wife walks into the room and sees him sitting there. "Raaph, what are you doing? I thought you said you were going to the shed to get some work done."

"Yeah," he says, never taking his eyes off the wall.

Chapter 5

"Well, what are you waiting for? Go and get your work done so we can spend some time together later tonight."

He doesn't move or say a word.

"Raaph, Raaph, what's wrong? I've never seen you this way before, never."

"I'm not upset, I'm just disappointed. I didn't want things to end this way."

"What do you mean my love?"

"Well, Kadesha, it's like this. I plan on creating children for us."

"Yes, I am well aware of that."

"Well it's hard when I know not all of them are going to choose to love us the way we love them. I am hurting inside for the children that I haven't even created yet and how they will reject our love and choose differently, oh so differently then what our original intent was. I don't want to create a place of torment. How could that ever be a place that someone would allow their loved ones to go?"

"Now, now my dear, you know you must, it's not a choice any longer. We both know what Lucarious is up to and we both know what he will do and you can't allow him to stay here. It would be the end of you... the end of us; all three of us can't be around evil. You knew that when you started this entire love story. You knew that there was a chance this would happen but you decided to create the kingdom citizens and our earthly children anyway. You knew that there was a risk involved; a chance that not all of them would love us, not all of them would see us for who we are. Of course it had to be Lucarious that started the entire thing. I warned you to be careful and not make him so beautiful with so many responsibilities. It was a risk that you were willing to take and now we must change the way things are going. You must continue with your work. The rebellion must be removed far, far away from us and our citizens."

"But he will deceive nations and nations will go with him and be tormented also."

"Here, here honey, you must not worry yourself to death. Think of all the possibilities that may happen. You knew that this was a chance when you created them with a will. Now you must love them so much that you allow them to make up their own minds. If they enter the rebellion and follow him, well they chose that, not you. Love without choices is no love at all. If you wanted everyone to love you no matter what, you shouldn't have given them free will. But you did and now you must allow them to decide where they want to spend eternity, with us or within the rebellion. It's up to them now. You must finish what you started."

"Do you understand that many will be deceived? He will deceive many and we will never see them again once their life force is empty and they pass along to the next world. How hard is it going to be without them in our lives? So many that come to live with us will have children in the rebellion or parents in the rebellion and when they come to live with

Chapter 5

us how do we respond, what will it be like for the kingdom citizens? How will they respond, how will they react? They have never seen pain, especially pain of their families choosing the rebellion and that they will never be allowed to see them again."

"Well my love, we will just have to devise a plan to take care of the pain.

"We have no pain in the kingdom nor can or should we allow it to grow in the kingdom."

"Now go and lie down and quit thinking about it, take some time and rest. You should rest."

"Yes, you are right. I will finish but not today. I will go and rest, then tomorrow I will restart." The king sighs a huge sigh. "Maybe tomorrow I will start, just not today." The very next day King Raaph wakes up and goes about his day as usual. He decides that after lunch he will go and create again. So he eats his breakfast and then heads for his throne. He enters the throne room and sits down. The worship team starts and the entire kingdom goes straight into worship. They love worship. They love to sing and dance for the king. They love the music that Lucarious plays. His songs that he writes are always so catchy everyone loves them and they stick inside their heads all day long. All the citizens catch themselves throughout the day singing. His song selection is just as amazing as his songs. He always picks the songs perfectly and it is always the right song for the right minute. Worship has always been something the entire kingdom has loved and would never miss no matter what. They sing many songs to their king whom they love and they know loves them. It seems to them they can feel the love radiating from him and into them during worship. They always walk home from worship feeling amazing. No matter what, they know that tomorrow will always start out with great worship time. The king heads into the palace and down to the dining area. Kadesha brings out a plate of food.

"So what is the special occasion?"

"What do you mean Raaph?"

"Well this is my favorite food; I wonder why you made it for me."

"Your favorite food? Tell me what food isn't your favorite." He looks up at her with a smile and they both begin to laugh. They laugh and laugh. King Raaph eats the food and after he finishes he lets out a big sigh.

"Now what?" Kadesha asks.

"What do you mean my dear?"

"What was the sigh for?

"Because I'm full I guess."

"Are you sure?"

"Yeah I'm sure. I guess I will go over and get to work."

"Ok, well have fun."

"Ha! Of course I'll have fun. I'm going to create us more children, earthly children. I am creating us children who will love us."

"What about what we talked about last night?"

Chapter 5

"Well it's like this, yes, you and I know that they will make mistakes and they will need to be forgiven. We know that, so we will make a way for that. So as far as we are concerned they are all forgiven for everything. All they have to do is believe that we made the way for them to be forgiven. Then be sorry for the mistakes they made and then ask to be forgiven. So in reality they are all forgiven before they do anything wrong. So we can see them as perfect, we can see them as the finished product. So it won't be hard."

"But they won't all love us back. What about that part?"

"Well that will be their decision. So since we won't make that decision for them, we see them as we created them, not as they ended."

"I guess you're right, we will look at them as the way we created them. Raaph, this will be a beautiful love story."

"Yes my dear, that is the plan."

King Raaph heads into the shed. He walks over and turns on the fan. Within a few minutes after he opens the shed up, a messenger citizen arrives with some incense from the altar.

"Lanama, please come in, how are you my friend?"

"Perfect, my king."

"Good, glad to hear it. Please take the incense and light it over there and there." Lanama walks over and places the fire that burns in the fireplace of the throne room on to the incense bowls. Soon the room is filled with a wonderful smell. No one could possibly smell anything else.

"Lanama?"

"Yes, my king?"

"Don't you just love that smell?" He breathes in deeply and breathes out. "Isn't it so relaxing?"

"Yes, my king, I think it is relaxing. So king, why are you working in here today?"

King Raaph looks up and hesitates as he isn't ready to reveal anything to the citizens yet. "I'm thinking about creating, I just love to create."

"Anything come to mind yet my king?"

"Well, truthfully, yes, I have a few different ideas but not sure which one to pick first. It should be fun either way."

"Well, my king, I guess I should leave you alone to work on your projects. Besides, today is the relay race practice for all the messenger citizens."

"Oh yes, you are right. Well come over here."

The king puts his hand on Lanama's shoulder. "I bless you, your muscles and your feet my child, may you do better than even you hoped and expect to do. Now be blessed and go race."

"Tha tha thank you my king!"

Lanama runs out of the room with the biggest smile on his face. He is speechless. It's not too often that the king puts his hands on anyone let alone encourages them to do better than they want to do themselves.

"Today must be my special day," he says to himself as he quickly heads to the practice races.

Chapter 5

The king is now alone and decides to open the book. As soon as he touches it, he sees in his mind Lucarious reading it. He just shakes his head. He sighs and says, "Lucarious, you're supposed to be my friend. Why are you spying on me? Oh well, not much I want do about it right this second."

He opens the book and starts to flip it to the last written page. There is a numbered check list. He wrote on the first day of creation, "Separate the darkness from the light." He also has written to make a difference between morning, noon, and evening. He also wrote make a difference between day and night. He thought to himself, "Well, that is done and it is good." The next thing he wrote was, "On the next day I decide to create, I will create water and sky. I will need to separate the sky from the water. I will need to make sure the water only goes so far. I also need to make it pleasing to the eye." He reread that and said to himself, "Well, that part is done and it is working perfectly." He moves on down the check list. He reads, "On the third day that I decide to create, I will have to make land and keep it dry for life to grow. The sky that is already separated from the water will also need to be separated from the land as that will also make it pleasing to the eye. The land on the earth has to be able to keep alive the plants and the trees. The trees and plants must be able to reproduce and make more of them. I will have to create a seed that can fall from tree and somehow have it grow in the ground. Well that is also is working out great. It works even better since I decided to create the wind. The fruit is either consumed or falls on the ground. The fruit then turns into a perfect place for the seed to start to grow."

He goes to the next one which is the number four. There he has written, "On the fourth day that I will create, I will separate which part of the earth will have light and which will have night at any given time. I should also make the earth go through different seasons, which will help the plants and the trees to recreate themselves. I need to make place for a star near the earth to keep it warm and give it light. I should also give the earth something to light up the night; it shouldn't have total darkness at night." He said to himself, that is done and it works well. The earth is perfectly spaced away from the sun. The path it travels helps the seasons work out perfectly. The moon stands in the presence of the sun all day and into it reflects the sun all night long." So on he reads. "The fifth day of creation, I should create living creatures that both fill the air and fill the water. I also want these animals to reproduce and fill the earth's land and its sea with many animals." He thinks to himself. "This is also done and it is all working well. They are reproducing and filling the sky and the trees very well. The sea is also filling up nicely." He continues to read. "On the sixth day of creation I will create the animals that walk the earth, including man. Well, I have already created all the animals and man. I already introduced the animals

Chapter 5

that will live outside the garden to the earth. Now I need to introduce the earth to man and the animals that will live inside the garden forever with man. I want man to rule over every animal and the earth. I will give every seed bearing plant for him to eat. The green leaf plants are reserved for the animals to eat and nourish them. He can do what he pleases with each animal. I will hold back man's mate, and allow him to live for awhile to see what it's like without her. Then since he will be strong and she will be loving, he will always remember what it was like without her. Then he should do everything to protect and cherish her. Well it seems that I still have some work to do."

The last thing on his check list is rest.

"The last day of creation will actually be eternity. I will go and rest and I will stay in rest forever. I no longer will need to be concerning myself with things, because I will be done and I will be at a restful peace forever."

He decides to go back to work. He walks straight back passing through the rooms and heads straight into the room full of stench. He grabs the mask and the suit, walking towards the work bench as he is trying to hop into the suit. After getting it all on, he can still taste the smell in his mouth.

"Well Lucarious, you were my pride and joy, you were my best friend. I am still hoping that you will understand what you are trying to accomplish just isn't possible. I wish that you would just realize that. Allow your pride that is in your heart to die because it has changed you. It has changed everything from your mindset to your attitude to your work ethic. You allowed it to rob the perfect life you had. I am surprised of all the citizens it would be you. You had the most and the most to lose. Now you want the only thing I won't give you, the only thing that I reserved for myself. Just change Lucarious, just change your mind and then I won't have to send you to this place I am now creating, the only thing that I ever created or ever will create that won't be pleasing, fun, or beautiful. This place will be full of pain and torment. This place is for you my friend; it's just going to be made for you. I know that you will deceive many and take them with you. That's not what I want, not what I planned. Unfortunately it's the way it is. The only good thing I can see coming out of this entire thing is the ones who stay and the ones who come to live with me will be the ones who want to be here. Nothing like this will ever happen again.

Ok, so where was I, where did I leave off? Oh yes, I was designing Horent. No one will enjoy one second in that heat."

So after he finishes that place of pure unhappiness, he takes a break. Removing the mask and the suit, he hangs it back on the wall.

Then he proceeds to go back to what makes him happy, his earthly children. He unlocks the filing cabinets and pulls out a book. He reads each name that is written on the pages. His wife walks in and asks, "What are you doing?"

Chapter 5

"I'm reading a book. It's an amazing book, if I do say so myself."

"What book is it?"

"It's called the perfect love story. It was written by a great author, King Raaph."

"Hahaha, you are the cutest Raaph! I sure do love you. So tell me what's in your book?"

"It is names of every earthly child we will have."

"And just how many earthly children will we have?"

"Just over fifteen billion."

"Fifteen billion? Did you really just say fifteen billion?" She looks for a seat as she feels like she will fall over. "Fifteen billion? Wwhy would you have that many children?"

"Just more to love and more to love us. Just remember love is never divided it only multiplies. When you gave birth to our son you didn't have to take half your love from me and give it to him did you?"

"No, no I didn't. I guess I didn't."

"Exactly! It multiplied. Love multiples, it grows and it is exciting."

"But how did you pick that number?"

"I just thought of different kids who all look different. They all are beautiful and none will be the same. They all will have different ideas, plans, and likes; they will all enjoy different things—which is perfect, because each thing will play off of the other. Then there will be no lack of anything on the earth."

"What do you mean?"

"I mean a few of my children will love plants so they will take care of the plants and the flowers for all the other children to enjoy. Some will realize that they may not like to clean up after a meal, and they will see that they can charge their brothers and sisters to clean up for them. Everyone will work in harmony and it will be perfect. They will pick a helper and fall in love with their helper. That will show them what it feels like to be you and me. We will visit them daily and it will be a great time by all."

"So why did you pick the number fifteen billion?"

"I didn't. I only had to create two. I am giving them creative power. Each child they create will be different looking and different all together different."

As his wife leaves the room, he sits at his desk and starts to read the name of every earthly child that is going to receive life. He already decided the exact day they will be created by their mother and father. He decided what hobbies and interests he has given to each one. As he is working on this, he makes sure their personalities are all different, especially for each family. He doesn't want each kid in each family to act or to look exactly like each other. He wants everyone to be unique and slightly different. In the back of his mind he sees the rebellion changing his original intent. Although his original intent was for them to live forever on the earth, he realizes that the rebellion is real and it has already begun. Although there is always time for forgiveness, Lucarious is about to step over the line of no return. At that point

Chapter 5

he says to himself, "This is why I have given them an end date as well as the beginning date. They can't live forever because of the choices they are going to make. There must be consequences for their actions."

Chapter 6

Although everyone thought that he went to the earth for a vacation, he decided that he would plant a garden. Since the rebellion had already begun, he won't be able to lovingly persuade a change of mind inside of Lucarious. So now earth will be the beginning and final destination of mankind's body. He remembers on the day that he decided to create he opened a bag and pulled out some clay. He remembers the day he dug the clay out of the earth. He remembers how he started to play with it, warming it up and adding just a little moisture to it so that it became bendable. Then he formed into a shape that looks like a miniature him. It has legs with feet; it has a round head on top, arms and a torso. Then next he sculpted out the toes and the nails. He started to draw the hair that will be on their heads. With every stroke of his hand, he breathed love on it. He continued to form the legs and shapes and the fingers. He then made the eyes. He sat the form down in the middle of the workbench and pulled out the charts that he had set aside. He worked and worked and

Chapter 6

worked, making every little part of this child's body work in harmony. Every system was created with love and care. He knew if they ate they wouldn't be able to use every part of the food. They needed to stay warm and they need to have blood going through their bodies. He created their stomach and all the other internal parts using the same charts that he used when he designed the kingdom citizens. They are built very similarly to each other. Now comes the most important part. He starts to work on their reproductive parts. They need to be able to reproduce.

"They will be able to fill the earth with all of my children. I will give them reproductive power but more importantly I will give them my own personal life force. I have never done that before. I will add my own life force to their blood. It will make them different from the citizens we already have. Every system inside of them must complement each other. They must work together in harmony for this body to work and stay alive. But not only will they have creative power to reproduce but to create things with their mind, to make things that will help them on the earth. They'll create things to make their jobs easier, ways to get around. Since they won't need to come to the kingdom, I did not give them wings or the ability to fly. They will have to learn how to create their own flight systems."

He continues to read his logs that he wrote as he created. "So now that I have made my earthly child I must name him. I think we should call him man.

The Chosen One

Man will start all of mankind. Yes, we will call our earthly children mankind, but each will need their own unique names. For now, I will create one and I will teach him everything he will need to know and how to be the ruler of the earth." He stops reading and decides it is time.

The king calls his wife and his son together. "Come, come quickly! See what I have been working on for the last few months, come and see."

"What is it father, what is it?"

"Well, my son, I call it man; it is the first of its kind and it will be our child and our friend. We will teach it all the secrets of the earth. We will give it the earth as its home and we will allow it to rule and reign on the earth."

"Is it like us father?"

"No, my son, it is nothing like us. We are much, much different, you will see."

"Is it like the kingdom citizens?"

"No, my son, it's not even anything like them."

"Father, whatever can it do?"

"I have given it the power to create and also recreate itself."

"Is it better than us Father?"

"No, son it's not, not at all."

"Well is it better than the kingdom citizens?"

"No, my son, I have created them to be our friends, but we will love and treat them as children. The citizens may travel to earth but mankind will not come to the kingdom. The earth is theirs to rule and

Chapter 6

reign forever. That is why I created the earth. Now let's all go down to the earth together and we will bring life to this creation I call man and introduce the earth to him."

All three of them leave the palace and head to the deck on the obsitorium. They are all excited and anxious to see this new creation and to see what it will be like. They all walk out to the edge of the deck. Both the king and his wife hold their son's hands and they jump toward the earth. When they get there they see that things look a little different from when they were there the last time. They notice that there is a garden that has some bushes on the outer edge that gives it a border like fence. They also see the king's zoo creatures are not entering and exiting the garden. They seem to be staying away from it. When the family walks through the entrance of this new garden that was planted by the king, they can tell that he planted it the last time he came to earth for a visit. Everyone wondered why he was gone so long the last time. This is it; this is the reason that the king spent so much time away from the kingdom on his last vacation. He wasn't vacationing; he was working on the garden. He was preparing it for the new life that he was about to introduce.

When they entered the garden, they suddenly realized that there were many new animals. These were some strange looking creatures walking around. They couldn't believe how small they were compared to the creatures outside the garden.

"Why are they so small and what is their purpose?"

"Father, what kind of animal is that and what is that thing's name?"

"Well, son, I decided not to name them yet. Since man will rule and reign on the earth, I decided to allow him to name the animals. That will be a fun day in paradise."

"What is paradise father?"

"Never mind my son. Never mind. Ok, well we walked long enough, this is where it will all happen, this is what I am going to call "The Garden". Man will live in the garden and the garden will produce food for his life force to be replenished. He will have to help it along and check it and make sure that everything is going smoothly. I will not overburden him with lots of hard work. I plan on his life being a gift, not a punishment. We will come and visit him daily so we can teach him and see how everything is going in his life."

"Father, you have brought us here many times but we never saw this place before. Is it new?"

"No, son, it's been here the entire time but I did change things. The last time I came for a visit, I actually came to finish this garden. The garden has been here, I just hid it from everyone's eyes; I didn't allow anyone to see it. I didn't want anyone to know about it nor did I want them to know about mankind."

"Why, father?"

"Yes, why so secretive?" Kadesha asks.

Chapter 6

"Well, I don't want there to be any problems. I want the citizens to find out together and I want to be the one to tell them, although it's not working like I wished it would. But nevertheless, it still is going to be a grand celebration in the kingdom when I reveal this creation. So everything looks perfect, just as I imagined it would look when I thought about creating the earthly children. The garden is ready and the fruit is ripe. The new animals are all well and doing fine. They are staying in the confines of the garden. They will be protected here in the garden. There is plenty of vegetation for food for the animals. They look well fed and happy."

"Father, why aren't the older animals in the garden? I only see the new animals."

"Well, son, I was hoping you wouldn't ask. I didn't put them in here because there will be changes coming to the kingdom and the earth. These changes aren't for the good. I knew this and I also knew that many, many years from now our children will need their bodies to get by on in their life. I really only ever created them to be a source of energy later on after the bodies go through many changes under the ground many years from now. I never intended for them to live forever. I created them for my children to use. That is why I created the earth. So they could do what they pleased, whatever they think is good; they own the earth. The earth doesn't own them."

The king walks them over to the middle and takes the clay that he has formed into a man that fits in his

The Chosen One

hand. He says to them, "Help me and we will make Jira together." They pull and stretch the clay. They bend and pull on the arms the legs and the feet. Then King Raaph takes a stick and breaks off the leaves and the pulls it from the tree. He shapes it till it is sharp. He then starts to make cuts between the toes and then on top the fingers. He starts sculpting the nails. He then starts to separate the lips with the sharp stick. Then he pokes holes for the ears and carves out the lobes. Next he carves the eyes. It is finished. He starts to move the lips apart. He opens the mouth, and stops, looking over at his son and wife.

"Are you ready?"

"Yes, father, we are! We are! Go do it, let's see it, hurry, hurry!"

King Raaph grabs a hold of the clay figure which is now as tall as the kingdom citizens.

He says out loud, "I command every system and every cell to come alive and work just as I designed. I command it work as we have planned it to be before the earth was created."

King Raaph takes a deep breath and holds it in. The king, the creator of all then places his lips on the clay formation. He begins to blow hard into the mouth and then, *kaboom!* Every system comes alive. The clay formation no longer looks like clay; it has color and starts to look much different. It starts to gasp for air just like it never had any wind in its lungs. After a second the lungs catch up with the body and he starts to breathe on his own. Now imagine you

Chapter 6

never existed before. The first thing you ever see in your life when you open your eyes for the first time is the creator of it all. You know nothing, you have no history, you just are alive. The creator stands there smiling and looks into the eyes of his creation. He says, "Jira, your name is Jira; you will be called Jira. I am King Raaph. I created you and you are my child. I will teach you everything you need to know and you will be my child and I will be your father. I promise to love you forever no matter what happens. Now I command your brain to start to speak immediately. Because it already knows my language and you already understand what I am saying."

Jira stands there just staring and blinking, not knowing what to do or what to say. So the king gives him a minute to get a grip. After he stops staring at the king, he moves his hands to in front of his chest. Lowering his head he stops and stares at his hands and then looks at the back of his hands. He turns his head and looks at his shoulders, his chest and his feet. King Raaph says again to him, "Your name is Jira. I am King Raaph. I created you, you are my child and I will teach you everything there is to know. Now follow me."

Jira immediately follows the three as they walk together to the lake. There the king has him kneel down and look into the water. He sees his reflection for the first time and jumps back. Raaph says, "It's ok, it's ok. It is Jira that you are looking at and now look again." Ever so slowly Jira moves toward the lake's reflection. He looks at himself and then moving his hands to his face, he touches his chin and then on to his cheek. He pulls at his cheek and then moves his hand to his hair. He smiles because the king has not stopped smiling at him. He realizes everything is good. Jira and the king stand up together. The king's his son and his wife spend the evening with Jira talking and teaching him everything there is to know.

Kadesha speaks up and reminds the king it is getting late. So the king tells his wife and son they need to go. They tell Jira, "This garden is your home. Stay inside the garden. You see the red bushes around the edges. No need to go past them, everything in here is yours and your home. Get some rest and relaxation. There will be much work for you in the coming days. You must learn many things and I also have some gifts for you." So Raaph walks him around and they pick up stones together. They make a circle and then the king grabs two branches off a tree. He bends them backwards and pulls off all the leaves. He then starts to rub them together until a flame starts. Jira jumps back and the king says, "No, it is good. It's ok. The fire will help you stay warm at night." He then grabs his hands and walks him to other trees with long leaves and they rip the branches off. They walk over to where the fire is and they make him a mat. King Raaph tells him to lie down and he obeys.

He says, "Sit here and have fun. Dark is coming and we must go. I will leave you until after the sun reaches that part of the sky. We will see you

Chapter 6

tomorrow, Jira. Have a great night." The king then says, "Ok, I'm ready." So they grab hands and jump and land back onto the deck of the obsitorium.

The king is interested to see what happened while all three were away. No one was informed of their departure. And everything seems to be in place as if they had never left. The citizens are all walking around doing their thing, getting ready for night to fall upon the kingdom. All three of them head to the palace and shut the door. They go straight to the kitchen and have a feast.

"It is good, it is good!" says Raaph.

Kadesha says, "Yes, I am very impressed, you did a great thing, nice job on your newest creation. It's probably one of your best."

"One of my best? It is my best!"

"Although it is not as strong or powerful as the citizens, it seems nice."

Raaph interrupts her and says, "It doesn't need to be powerful, it just needs to be loved. That is how I designed it, to be loved and to hunger after love. I also designed it with a strong desire to also worship."

"Father?"

"Yes, my son?"

"Why doesn't man have the power of flight? Why does it look so different from the citizens? It looks more like you and me."

"Well, son, as I told you before it doesn't need flight; our children will not be coming here for a visit. We must visit them. That is the plan. That is the idea.

Every evening we will all three go down and walk and talk and teach the children how to live and how to love. We will teach them who they were created to be and how to love everything and how to respect everything. We will teach them how to rule and reign. There is a way to rule and reign and take control over all the earth without hurting it. We must teach them how to respect it because it must remain their home."

The next day the king goes about and has a normal day in his kingdom. No one seems to be the wiser to what he is doing on the earth. He can hardly wait to reveal what he has been working on to the cities. They will definitely be intrigued. So when it is closer to the late afternoon, he goes and finds his wife and his son.

"Come with me, we must go back to the earth. We will see what Jira has been up to all day."

"Father?"

"Yes, my son?"

"Well if you are the creator of all and you know everything about everyone, why should we go and see what he did? Don't you know already?"

"Well, sort of."

"Sort of? How could you not know what he did all day?"

"Well my son, you know how you love to draw me pictures?"

"Yeah."

"Well when you draw them for me, they are a gift to me, correct?"

"Yes, father, that is correct."

Chapter 6

"Well I want them to be a surprise to me as well. I don't want to know what my gift is before you give it to me, so I block it from my mind."

"Block it? How could you possibly do that?"

"I can do anything I want, my child. I block it so it will be a surprise and I will love it even more if it is a surprise. I will block things from my mind so that they are a surprise. No more delays, let's go."

The king and his family travel from the obsitorium to the earth. They gently land on the ground and quickly spot Jira.

"Jira, come, come and spend time with us."

"Oh King, oh I'm so glad to see you. The fire you made me is gone, it disappeared. I'm sorry I fell asleep and it was gone. Please forgive me."

"No worries, Jira, the fire is not gone. No fire that I ever created will ever go out. The fire is still there, it is just so small it is hard to see. We will make it large again. Before I leave, it will be back for you to keep warm. So tell me, my child, how was your first day? How do you like your home?"

"Oh, I love it! It is nice. I love looking at everything. I didn't do much last night. I just sat in front of the fire and played with it. It was a lot of fun. Eventually I fell asleep. When I woke up, everything was so bright and loud. These things that sit up high, they make nice noises, and I like to listen. Then I walked around and there are things that walk around too. But they don't look like me and they don't talk to me. I don't know why they don't talk. I tried to

The Chosen One

get them to talk, but most ran away from me. So I chased them and they ran away. It was fun. I like it here. I wish you were here. I don't know anyone else. I wasn't sure what I was supposed to do today."

"Well, Jira, you weren't supposed to do anything. I just want you to be, just be."

"Well, how can I just be when I don't know what to be?"

"Just be, Jira, just be. Just be yourself and love. Love is the most important thing. Love everyone and everything. Respect everything and don't hurt on purpose. I gave you the entire earth for you to rule and reign over, but you must do it in a way that you respect all things and love all things. Then life with be easy for you."

"Ok, king, I will do that. I will."

"Now, Jira, I have a fun day planned for all of us. We are going to watch you name every creature that I have created. So let's find a nice rock to sit on. I will call the animals to come to us. Together we will see what you will call each one of them. I am excited to see what you will name them."

"Me, name them? Oh no, I couldn't do that. You name them, you created them. That's ok, I'll sit back and watch you king. You name them."

" Hahahaha! That's so nice of you but I am giving this job to you."

"But ...but...I...uh...I...uh, don't how to do that. I don't know what to call them. I have no idea what to say. I'm not sure where to begin."

Chapter 6

"Jira, that's no problem, just say whatever you think. Say whatever comes to your mind. Say how they make you feel. Let's begin."

So King Raaph calls each animal one by one to his side. He pets and holds on to each as Jira tries to come up with names. "This one is white and fluffy. What do you think Jira?"

"I call it a lamb."

"Nice, I like that name. How about this one?"

"Oh, it's a wolf."

"What do you think about this one?"

"How about bird? Since it is blue it is a blue bird. And that one is a cardinal and an eagle and a hawk and a sparrow and a dove."

"Wow! You are doing great, I'm proud of you my child. Now, what about that one?"

"Um, it's a pig, and that will be a cow and a horse."

"What about this one?"

"That's a s s s snake. Yes, we will call that a snake. This one will be a bison and that is a buffalo. This is fun, King Raaph, and it's easy, so easy. The names are fun. I could do this all day."

"Don't worry Jira, we have many more animals to name. We will be here a while." After the last animal came forward to be name he called it the duckbilled platypus because he was running out of names.

King Raaph says, "Now let's all go for a walk."

So Raaph walked his family all along the edges of the garden. He explained that this was called a border and that there was no reason for Jira to leave.

Immediately Jira said, "Ok, I won't. But what will happen if I do leave?"

Raaph says, "Nothing. Nothing would happen to you, but there is no reason to leave. I placed everything that you would ever need inside this border that we are walking. Nothing bad would happen, I am just saying there isn't a reason to leave. But before I rekindle the fire, I have one more animal to show you. One more name."

"Oh king, I can't. I completely ran out of names. I couldn't possibly name one more animal. I am drained of names."

King Raaph laughs out loud and says, "Just one more, then I will go home for the night. The darkness of the night is fast approaching and you need your sleep."

So they walk over to the edge of the garden. They stand at the entrance and they look out into the rest of the world. They see these huge animals running around and chasing each other. Some are young and others are old.

"Jira, take a good look at these animals and name them well. But more importantly, take a good look at them for their time is short on the earth. They won't live much longer."

"Why? Where are they going?"

"Well my child, they were created for a purpose. Some day the earth will depend on them as a natural source from the earth. It is my gift to the future."

"Well they look like dinosaurs to me."

Chapter 6

"So be it. We will then call them dinosaurs. That's a great name. Dinosaurs it is. Now let's get that fire going so I can leave and you can rest after that long day."

The king and his family return to the kingdom and again the citizens haven't even noticed that anything was out of place, that the king was disappearing in the evening and no one really seemed to be looking for him or his family. So they traveled back to the palace and settled in for the night. That night the king lay in his bed and closed his eyes. He could feel something was different. Something was not the same. So he opens his eyes. His wife was looking at him. She was smiling, watching him. "What is it my dear, what is wrong?"

"Oh, nothing is wrong."

"Then why aren't you falling asleep and resting? You know that the days are busier than ever. We have much to do tomorrow, so please rest now, Raaph."

"Yes, my dear."

"When are you going to give Jira a wife?"

"A wife? I don't know, eventually, when the time is right I guess. I'm not sure yet. We will see how things go. Not everything is planned out step by step, day by day. I like to let things happen and have things flow together. It's nice because it always works out well."

"You know Raaph it's not good for him to be alone," Kadesha reminded him. "It would be better

The Chosen One

if he had someone to talk to and spend time with while we are gone."

"Kadesha, he isn't alone. He has the entire earthly animal creation to live with, spend time with and enjoy. That should be enough for now."

"If you say so Raaph, but I think that his life would be more enjoyable with a wife, some one for him to talk to and to spend time with. But since you think the animals are enough, then I want you to show me the one animal that he will befriend and spend his life with…every waking moment. Which one will bring him the joy that I bring to you? You did say there will be many children and the earth someday will be full."

"One day at a time, my love, one day at a time. We will see; take it one day at a time and when the time is right we will introduce his mate to him."

The next late afternoon the king and his family head back to the obsitorium. They again leave for earth and gently land in the garden and immediately look for Jira. They see him chasing some of the animals around and immediately wonder what is wrong, so they go to investigate. They stop just as they start to get close and realize that Jira is laughing hysterically while chasing the animals. Some he catches up to and taps them on their back and runs away. Others he tries his hardest to catch but they are just too fast for him. The king thoroughly enjoys watching this; in fact the entire family is having a blast just watching. They stand there just smiling away, laughing and having a great time.

Chapter 6

Jira cuts the corner too fast and falls. As he catches his breath and stands up, he realizes that his king is watching him and he stops for a second. He looks into their eyes. Jira sees them smiling from ear to ear and sees the love in their eyes. He realizes that they are happy with what they just caught him doing. He was kind of embarrassed but now realizes that it is ok.

"Having fun?" the king yells to Jira. So Jira decides to jog over to the king's family.

"So, Jira, tell us, how was your day? Did you enjoy the day and the planet which I created for your enjoyment?"

"Oh, yes, my king, very much so. I followed all the animals around and I watched them. I watched them and I think I know them a little better. I know what they like and what they don't want. I know what their favorite foods are. I like how they group together in the evening and make tiny little families, then go to sleep. They seem to enjoy each other and like to stay that way in the evenings. I like how they look for food for the littlest ones. I like how they teach the little ones how to find food and what they should eat, how to walk and how to jump. It's been a great day. I was surprised, I didn't think that I would remember all their names but I did. I did remember each ones' names and as I saw each one today, I reminded them that that was their name. They seemed to like their name also and seem to respond to it when I call them that. The animals seem pretty smart. What you created here in the garden is good."

The Chosen One

"Yes, Jira, I agree it is good. So what are you going to do tomorrow?"

"I, uh, I, uh, I don't know."

"Well my son, I think that you should take care of the garden and the earth for that matter. I think that you should look at the plants and study them."

"Study them? What is that? What is study?"

"Well, Jira, that is what you did today. You studied them and learned things about them. Now I want you to do that again. But this time do it with the trees. Then you can study the shrubs and bushes. You can work your way down to the flowers. They need love, too. I created all of creation to need love. You discovered that the animals enjoy your company and they like when you spend time with them and when you talk to them. The vegetation is the same, it loves when you talk to it. It will only grow better and come more alive as you help it. I gave you hands and a brain. I gave you the ability to think and the plant life has no arms; so if the limbs need help or adjusted, well, then do it. Adjust them and you may even have to cut and trim them from time to time."

"Cut them? You mean like when you pulled off the tree limbs to make me a fire?"

"Yes, Jira."

"But will it hurt?"

"Yes, my child, it will hurt them and does hurt them when they are removed."

"I don't understand my king, why would I want to hurt them?"

Chapter 6

"Well, Jira, things will need your help, they are not perfect. They grow and reach for the sun so they can keep growing but that isn't always good. If you prune and cut it will only make them stronger and sturdier. Pain isn't always a bad thing. Always remember I have given the earth to you, it is yours to do as you please. A gift means I no longer have control over it because it belongs to you. But I expect you to take care of it and show it love. Every decision you make will have consequences, but, over all, you are in control. If you take care of the earth it will take care of you."

So the king and his family start to get ready to go back to the palace. They see Jira watching and looking at the animals, still studying them and getting to know them.

Kadesha says, "Look Raaph, just look at him." They look over and see Jira sitting on a rock smiling from ear to ear just waiting and watching. "Have you found him a help mate yet."

"No, my dear, I haven't found anything or anyone worthy of him."

"The animals can't be it. Well? What are you waiting for?"

"Don't worry, I already created him a help mate. I just haven't shown her to anyone yet."

"Why didn't you bring her already?"

"Because I wanted everything about her to be a gift. I wanted him to realize what life was without her. That she will be the missing half. That he wasn't complete until he met her. I want him to love and cherish her, to guard and protect her. She will not be as strong as he is, so I want him to guard her and pay attention to her. Not to ever take her for granted. She needs to be loved just as he needs to be loved."

"Well, Raaph, let's take care of it now. Look at this." The king looks over at his creation, watching and studying all of the other creation. As he watches the animals pair back up and start bedding down for the night, he sighs. He thinks that it is nice, very nice. They all sleep in groups.

"Come, Jira, come over here."

Jogging over to him while trying to keep an eye on the animals, he says, "Yes, my king what is it?"

"Well, Jira, I want you to reignite the embers before I leave. I wouldn't want you to be cold tonight after the sun is completely gone."

"Yes, my king. I will go and do it right away."

"Good Jira, don't forget tomorrow you must work the trees and the plants and make sure all is well with them. Oh, there is one more thing. Walk with me my son."

They walk and walk for awhile until they are in the center of the garden.

"See that tree my child?"

"Yes, yes I do."

"Well my child, that is what I call the forbidden tree. Whatever you do, never eat from this tree. You may eat from all the other trees, but not this one. The fruit from the trees is what I created for you to be your food. All fruit is good for you and your body. It all tastes good. But I also need to know that you trust me, love me and understand that I have your best interest in mind. So I created this as the only one in which you may not eat from. Just leave it alone and all will be well."

"Father?"

"Yes, my child?"

"What will happen if I don't obey you?"

"Well, my son, you will know good and evil. Right now you only know good. That's all you ever need to know. Evil has nothing for you. So if you eat of it you will die."

"What exactly is death?"

"Well, you will go to sleep and never wake up. That will be it, life will be over."

"Huh, well it doesn't sound fun; I like my life so far."

"Well, Jira, it will only get better from here. I promise; so please just listen, ok?"

"Yes, father, I will obey. I don't need it. I have too many others to choose from."

"Yes, you do, Jira, yes you do. And that is a perfect way to think."

Chapter 7

The king and his family head back and they walk straight to the palace.

"Father?"

"Yes, my son."

"How long are we going to keep mankind a secret?"

"Well son, just a few more days, and then we will have a celebration. We will show every citizen what we have done, what we have been working on."

"Do you think they will like it father?"

"Yes, I do, what's there not to like my son?"

"Ok, father, I will see you tomorrow."

"Have a great night son."

"Raaph, you should really do something soon about his help mate."

"I know. I just want to teach him everything before I introduce her. That way he will already be on his schedule of maintaining the earth and will already have a routine down. Then when she comes, she can help him every step of his way. He can teach her. Then they can teach their children together. It will be a great time on earth."

Chapter 7

Meanwhile Jira peels off a few branches and then walks toward the fire. He breaks them into pieces and places some on the fire. He notices that he pulled branches from the tree. He also notices that the fire is changing the earth underneath the fire. He notices that he is able to change the earth. He gets up when the sun comes out. He starts to walk around and talk to the trees and the plant life as he goes on his day, looking, inspecting and changing anything he feels necessary.

Then he comes across that tree. The forbidden tree. He thinks to himself, "I never want to eat from that tree, not even by accident." So he finds two big rocks that are black in color. He rolls those rocks until they are directly in front of the tree. "Well, it's almost evening; the king should be here soon."

"Jira, Jira where are you?"

"I'm over here, my king."

The king and his family walk over towards Jira. "What are you doing?"

"I'm talking to the plants."

"So you figured it out, did you?"

"Yes, my king, when I talk to them, they change."

"You catch on very quickly my child. Great job. You are learning fast and very well. So walk with me and tell me more."

Jira starts to walk through the garden with the king and talk and explain to him every little thing he figured out earlier that day. The king also stops and shows him that he can even change the flow of the rivers by moving a few rocks.

"There is so much for you to learn, be taught and figure out yourself. Jira, you need to start to think about building a place for yourself."

"What do you, mean build a place?"

"Well, my child, at night you are sleeping on a bed of leaves. In the hottest part of the day you have to rest under a tree for shade; so I would like for you to have a place to go into, a place that would be all your own. None of the animals will live there with you. This will be a place for you to stay when you need rest or shade. Speaking of shade, when the sun is at the top of the sky, that is when the earth is the warmest. That part of the day is when the sun is closest to you. Make sure that you don't spend the entire day out in the open; and make sure that you are drinking water from the stream. You need water to replenish what you lose. Just like you need food to keep you going; you also need water."

"Ok, my king, I will do that and I will make sure that I drink lots of water."

"Let's go and figure out a shelter for you to live in."

The king shows him how he can build a shelter that can support a fire inside it. He can build a roof around the fire, one that will not catch the roof on fire. He explains that the sticks and twigs and leaves all have water inside just as he does. He also explains how the fire is hot and it makes the water leave the leaves and sticks.

"The fire then can burn very, very easily with all the water gone out of whatever you are trying to

Chapter 7

burn. This is why you must pay attention to what is close to the fire."

King Raaph takes some leaves and places them near the fire.

He says to Jira, "Watch this."

He neatly places them on the outer edge of the fire. He then adds some fuel to the fire. The fire gets even hotter than it was. Although the leaves aren't anywhere near the fire, they begin to smoke and burn. Then *woosh* they catch on fire.

"See, Jira, this is what I was talking about. This is what I meant when I say to be careful."

"Yes, my king, I will be careful."

They continue to find some nice rocks. They place some huge leaves and grass beside the rock.

"The rock will provide you a back wall. The leaves and grass will provide you a nice and comfortable bed. You can lie here all night."

They build a fire ring. He then teaches Jira about air flow and how the fire must breathe. Together they make a perfect ring of stones. He also explains how the fire weakens the stone.

He says, "After many days you will notice the stones are crumbling apart. You will have to change them out for new ones."

"When?" asks Jira.

"Not for a long, long time. But beware that when the stones begin to crumble, you need to replace them within a few days. Otherwise they will no longer keep you safe. Their life will be up."

The rocks they choose for the back wall also had two nice trees in front of them. They take some vines and tie the vines to the trees. They stretch the vines over top of the living space and set them on top of the back wall rocks. They place some heavy rocks on top of the rocks keeping the vines in place.

"That will hold the vines for you my child."

"Great, thanks, my king."

"Now gently place some leaves on top of the vines and these vines will keep them from falling onto you. It's a support system."

"Wow, king, you sure do know a lot. You thought of everything."

The king stops and smiles and laughs. "Yes, Jira, I did. I really did. I spent many hours designing your planet and even more designing you. There are many systems inside you that must all work together to keep you alive and to walk and talk, to see and also to hear."

"Wow! Will I ever be as smart as you?"

The king laughs again. "Yes, my child I will teach you everything I know. Now let's move the fire."

They both walk over to where they started the original fire. They take some sticks and catch them on fire. They walk the fire to the shelter. They light the wood that is already in the fire ring and waiting for them to return. They get the fire going and then they throw the sticks they used to start it into the fire. Once they are sure the fire will continue, they walk

Chapter 7

back to the original fire. They find some huge leaves and fold them up.

"Now watch this."

King Raaph walks over to the stream. He then dips his leaf cup into the stream and fills it up. Jira copies his king's actions. When both are full, they remove them from the stream and carry them to the fire. They take the water and pour it out, putting out the fire.

"Jira, always remember if you are done and never plan on using the fire again, then put it out. Fire and water don't mix; so always put out a fire that won't be used anymore. Also, keep water away from a fire that you plan on using. Well, my child, I must gather my family and head home, it is getting late."

"Ok, thanks again."

"Sure, my child, sure."

"Kadesha, Kadesha, where are you?"

"I'm coming, I'm coming."

"What do you have there?"

".... It's a picnic basket."

"I can see that, what's in it?"

"Food."

"What kinda food, Kadesha?"

"It's a pic; I want to have a picnic with our earthly child. Besides, aren't you the one that says everything changes when you eat a meal together?"

"Yes, my dear, I do say that. But you must be careful not to spoil him. There is no food like we have in the kingdom located anywhere on earth."

"I know, but I feel like feeding him."
"It's ok because I can use it."
"What do you mean you can use it?"
"Never mind."
"Don't tell me to never mind, I want to know."
"Well just wait, you will see. I'll meet you at the obsitorium. I have to get something. See you there," Raaph says as he is heading out the door.

"Come on son, we have to meet him there, let's starts walking." They get there and are only waiting a few minutes till they see the king walking towards them.

"What do you have there Raaph?"
"It's a box."
"I can see that, what's in the box?"
"It's a secret."
"There will be no secrets in our kingdom."
"Hahahhaha, I know, you will find out in a few minutes when we get there. Just wait and see; it's something you've been wanting and waiting for, for a long time."

"Oh, really? I can hardly wait."
"Let's go. We need to arrive quickly; there is much work to do. Ok, everyone ready?"
"Yes."
"Ok, grab hands." They jump down and softly land on the earth.

"Jira, oh Jira, where are you my child?"
"I'm coming. Give me a minute." Jira runs over and rinses his hands off in the river. Then he jogs over to the king and his family.

Chapter 7

"King, I didn't expect you, it seems earlier than usual."

"Yes, my child, I came early today. We wanted to dine with you. I expect you haven't eaten yet and are hungry."

"Yes, very hungry, my king. I didn't gather up enough food for us to eat. I will need to get some more, where should I meet you?"

"No need for that my child; we brought food from the kingdom."

"Really? Wow, I sure am excited! I never thought I would get anything from the kingdom; you said we were separate. So I never expected this. But I sure am excited to eat with my king."

"Go get the food that you gather. We will start with that since we shouldn't waste the fruit of the earth."

"Ok, I'll be right back." So Jira runs over and picks up the food. As he is walking back he drops some a few times.

The king says, "Well Jira, I think we should teach you how to build something to carry your food in."

"That sounds great, but I really don't mind making a few trips."

"Nonsense my child, soon you will have to gather up much more. You will need more food, much more food."

"King, am I going to start to feed the animals? They seem to be doing a good job by themselves."

Belly laugh. "Hahhaha! No, my son, not the animals. Your family, you will need to feed your family.

It will be your job to take care of and love each and every child that comes from you and your wife. But let's stop talking and eat."

Jira's heart is pumping so loud he can hardly think, let alone hear anyone talking. All he can think is, "What's a wife and what is he talking about and how will I have children? I don't understand."

"Jira. Jira? Jira!"

"Huh? Wah, what? Uh, yes, my king?"

"Please my child, stop concerning yourself with everything. Let's eat, and talk and eat some more."

Jira stopped dead in his tracks, suddenly for the first time he realized that King Raaph knew his thoughts. All he could do is stare.

"Please eat. Think later."

"Oh, ok, my king, I will."

As soon as they finish eating, Jira asks, "Can you tell me now my king?"

"Yes, I can, wait a minute."

Kadesha interrupts, "We haven't had the pie yet."

"Well you start to cut it up and I'll explain everything. Then we will all eat together."

"Ok." She reaches over and grabs the pie and the pie cutter. "Hand me the plates, my son."

"Ok, Mother. Here you go."

"Thank you, my son."

"Jira, we have decided that you need to have a mate, just like the animals. There are both male and female animals. As you can see, they reproduce. That is how they have little ones that look like them. They

Chapter 7

are called children. There will be many animals both male and female. Eventually this garden will have to be expanded all over the entire earth. So after thinking about who could be your mate, we decided to make another earthly child. This next child will be the last earthly child I ever create. I will give her to you and you two will create many children and you two will love them and teach them all they need to know, just as I have done with you. Then they will leave the shelter that you have built and they too will have children and they will also love them. Eventually, earthly children will cover the entire earth. We are going to introduce her today."

He takes the lid off of his box and Jira sees what seems to be a small version of himself made out of clay.

Raaph shuts the lid and says, "That is what you looked like before I breathed life into you."

Jira just sits there not knowing what to say or do. The king reaches down and hands his son a plate of pie, then places one in front of himself. He reaches down and picks up another, leaving one left in front of his wife. With the last piece in his hands, he pulls it up to his lips; he takes a deep breath and blows on the piece of pie. Then he looks at Jira and smiles. He hands it to Jira.

At this point, Jira is really confused and his brain is swimming with information overload. He smiles back and places the pie in front of him. He then takes his fork and cuts a piece off and then places it in his mouth. His taste buds explode inside his mouth and his eyes become huge. He chews and chews and chews. He says, "This is amazing! I thought the fruit I have is good, but this is incredible!" They continue to talk about what the king expects from Jira. The king continues to smile as he keeps looking back at his wife. Soon after, Jira starts bobbling his head while he is talking. He can't stop yawning. His eyes are heavy and his eye lids have become slits. Then *boom,* he falls over and hits the ground. At least he was still sitting, so he didn't have far to go.

King Raaph reaches down and picks his limp body up and carries him to a huge stone, lays him completely flat and then walks over to the box. He picks up the box and carries it over and then places it beside Jira. He then reaches down, opens the lid and pulls out a surgical scalpel. Then Kadesha and his son come quickly to investigate.

"Raaph, what have you done and what are you doing?"

"Well, my love, I am going to remove his bottom rib. Then we will place it in her and then I will breathe life into her. When he wakes up, he will meet his mate."

"Why must you do that?"

"Because her heart will be different than his. I am using part of his body to be a protector of her heart. Every time he sees the scars, he will remember that he is to protect her, love her, and never harm her. He should never allow anything to harm her. They

Chapter 7

both will realize her heart is different and her heart requires much more protection. Now help me stretch her out. Let's do exactly as we did with Jira."

He places the knife beside Jira. He reaches back into the box and pulls out the other clay figure he has made.

"Help me."

They all begin to pull and tug and help her take her shape.

"Let's make her just a little shorter than Jira."

When they get her exactly as they want her to look, they lay her down beside Jira. The king reaches down and cuts just below his ribs. He reaches in and slices off the bottom rib on each side. He places his hands on each side over top of each incision. He keeps them there and reaches down. He then blows gently on each side. The bleeding comes to a complete stop. He pulls apart her chest and places the ribs on the bottom of her rib cage. He forms them and attaches them to the others. He then pulls the clay stomach over the ribs. He forms it with his hands and then plays with it until no openings can be seen any more. He then repeats what he said over Jira over this next creation. He commands every cell and every organ to begin to come alive and to work as it was designed to operate. He then opens the mouth of the clay figure and takes a deep breath, holds it and places his lips over her mouth. He breathes out, filling her lungs with his air.

Between his breath and his life force, she becomes alive. She suddenly takes three steps backwards and bends over and starts to cough and cough and cough. Her lungs quickly fill up and she catches her breath. She stands straight up and sees the king and his family smiling and staring at her. She jumps back and lets out a *woooh*. She freezes. She's scared and doesn't know whether to run or what to do. The king puts out his hand and says, "It is ok. Come here, we want to talk to you. It's ok." She steps back.

Kadesha says, "Let me try." She gently walks toward her. She smiles and gently talks to her. She gently places her arm around her shoulder. She then gently walks her toward the king and her son. "It's ok, we know you are scared. We are sure this is scary for you, but everything is fine. You can talk just like I am talking to you. We are your family. We created you and you are made in our image. We have many things to show you and tell you." They all slowly sit her down on a rock. They explain to her what is going on. She quickly falls in love with her new family. She is so tender hearted that everyone who meets her can't help but fall in love with her.

So after a few hours of explaining what has been going on, they tell her it is time to meet Jira.

Kadesha asks Raaph, "What are we going to call her?"

He looks at her and smiles. He says, "That, my dear, that I am going got leave up to Jira."

They decide that they want to have her hide behind a large tree. They ask her to go and hide. They ask her to stay put and not come out until they call for

Chapter 7

her. They walk her to the tree. Then they all walk over to the stone where Jira is still unconscious. They go over and King Raaph places his hand over Jira's heart. He starts speaking to Jira. He calls his name until Jira comes around and comes to. Jira realizes he is lying down and sits up very quickly, almost too quickly. He suddenly feels pain for the first time in his life. He lets out an *awwwhhh*, takes in a deep breath and holds it. He lets it out.

He does that a few times then says, "What happened to me?"

Raaph says, "Jira, do you remember when I said pain isn't always a bad thing?"

"Yes," he says, holding his gut.

"Well, I put you to sleep and then I opened up your chest. I sliced off your two bottom ribs."

Jira is still breathing heavily and holding it and then letting it out. He is finally getting a sense to him and he turns and slowly stands up, never letting go of his gut. He says, "Wa wa whyy would you do that? And why does this hurt so badly, what's wrong?"

Raaph says, "Well, my child, just like the animals all have a mate and someone to spend time with, someone to sleep beside and someone to care for, I decided it was your time. Now you have a mate and I used part of you to make her, just as I used part of me and part of this earth to make you. She, too, was made in my image and she, too, has my life force flowing through her entire body."

The pain is quickly decreasing. As it lessens, now he can stand straight up and look King Raaph in the eye.

He says, "Well, where is my mate? Where is she, when can I meet her?"

"As you are ready, you can meet her, my child."

"Well, I'm ready. I sure am ready."

"Kadesha send her out." Kadesha walks behind the tree and then pushes the shy, beautiful young woman out from behind the tree. She walks out with a shy half smile on her face. She slowly walks toward him. Jira's eyes turn huge. No one could see or ever tell at this moment in time that he ever had eye lids. All he can do is stand there with his mouth open and eyes wide open and stare at her. She slowly, shyly walks up to him and touches his face, gently pushing his mouth shut. They both stand there starring at each other, unable to move. She reaches her hand out and places it into his hand. He is still frozen. He can't move. He has never seen anything like her.

"King?"

"Yes, my child."

"I think this is the most beautiful creation you ever made."

Not daring to take his eyes off of her for one second, half afraid that she will disappear if he even blinks, he squeezes her hand not realizing what he is doing. Kadesha walks up to him and places her hand on his shoulder and says, "Not too hard Jira. Be gentle. Be very, very gentle. She is not entirely like you. She

Chapter 7

is soft spoken and soft to touch. Be careful, always remember to be careful with her. Her heart is bigger than yours and you must at all costs guard her heart."

"Yyye, yeeea, yes, I will, I will. I promise I will!" He slowly eases up on her hand.

King Raaph says, "Well you two, my family and I must go. It is getting late. We must return to the kingdom and go to the palace for some rest. We will be back tomorrow as usual. We will check up on you two tomorrow and see how you two are doing tomorrow.

Jira?"

"Yes, King Raaph?"

"Take the day off tomorrow and take time to walk her through the garden and show her everything, and the different plants and the animals."

So Jira walks his new found friend around the garden pointing out some things. He asks her if she is hungry. She says, "I'm not sure, but I think so."

He says, "Well that's no problem. When we want to eat, we just go and pick some fruit from one of the trees and we eat it.

She notices a tree with a big black rock in front of it. She starts to walk toward the tree. It seems different. This tree seems to shine. It seems as if it draws you towards it. Jira is still walking and explaining things, not realizing that she has her eye on that particular tree. When they get very close to the tree she was eyeing up, she runs over and jumps up on the rock.

She yells, "Look this one. It already has some rocks for us to stand on so that we can reach the fruit up high."

Jira yells, "No! Stop!"

She freezes.

"Don't move."

He runs over to her.

"Stand still, stand very, very still." She doesn't know what to do or what to make of what he is saying. When he is close to her, he reaches up and grabs her hand and gently leads her off the rock. He walks her away from it and then turns around.

She says, "What's wrong, Jira?"

"Well, King Raaph told me that was the only tree we couldn't eat from. So pick another tree to eat from."

"Ok, but I don't understand."

"Well neither do I," he says. "I just know that he told me that I could eat the fruit from any tree except that one. So don't even touch that tree. Do you understand me?"

"Why shouldn't we?"

Jira cuts off her off before she finishes her sentence. "Because we will die, he said we will die if we do, so don't, ok. Come on."

Jira starts to lead her away from that tree. They find another tree that has beautiful ripe fruit and they eat from it.

"Jira?" She asks.

"Yes?"

Chapter 7

"What does it mean we will die?"

"Well, King Raaph told me that me that where we live is inside a garden on the planet earth. He refers to the ground as earth. He says as we begin to have children and the animals have children we will need to grow the garden. Come on."

So he walks her to the entrance of the garden. He points out that there is a huge world outside the garden where they live. He says someday the garden will completely take over the entire earth. "It will be our job to grow the garden and make this happen. So we must live forever."

They see some dinosaurs running around chasing each other. He points and says that they are alive. Then he finds one that is lying on the ground.

"Tonight you and I will fall asleep. We will lie on the ground like that one is over there. Our bodies will rest and then tomorrow we will wake up, and rise up and go to work again. But that one over there, I am pretty sure that one has died. That one looks like it is sleeping, but it's too early for sleeping. He is never going to wake up again. It will be over for him. No more life.

Well it's getting dark; we should go and get the fire going. It gets much cooler the darker it gets. The fire will keeps us warm all night."

He walks them back to the shelter. She is impressed that he already set up a place for them to live. He shows her the roof to keep them from the hot afternoon sun. He shows her the comfortable bed that was built to sleep on and the fire ring. He shows her how to stoke the fire. He shows her it never really goes out. It must be restoked and brought back. She feels like there is so much to learn. She feels like she loves Jira and sees that he is very smart. She also feels that he has a desire to take care of her. She can tell that he cares about her and her feelings. This makes her feel important. As the evening sun goes down, they sit around the fire and talk for hours. Jira realizes they have stayed up way too late and tells her they should rest. He lets her lie down on the bed. He lies down beside her and snuggles in towards her. They keep each other warm as the fire slowly dwindles down.

The very next day they wake up and Jira realizes how long they did stay up. He feels like they should get a quick start to the day. He runs over to the closest tree and then grabs breakfast for them. He walks over and wakes her up. He helps her to her feet and then gives her breakfast. After sleeping in and eating, Jira wastes no time taking her through the garden, teaching her how to fold leaves and make cups to drink with. He shows her how to prune a tree. He shows her how to make the river go where he wants it to go by moving a few rocks around. He introduces her to all the animals. He finds all the birds for her to see. He also does his best to find the fish hiding in the river. He teaches her all their names. He tells her how he got to choose their names.

He realizes that she has no name.

Chapter 7

He says, "We need to pick out a name for you. I think we should call you Tamum. I think that name fits you well. Soon the king will be coming."

He points to where the sun is.

Then he points to another part of the sky and says, "When the sun moves to that spot over there, that's when you can expect the king to come for his daily visits."

"What will happen then?" she asks.

"Oh, it's always different every day, but one thing I can promise you is it is always fun. Some days he teaches, other days we play games. He and his family are always fun to spend time with. They are all so nice to me. I think he will probably want to spend time talking and teaching us new things."

The sun finally hits that part of the sky. They are already waiting in the field where he always gently lands on the earth. The entire family soon comes and begins to walk with the new family. King Raaph told them that he decided there would be plenty of time to teach, so they should all just spend time together and just become family. His desire was for everyone to really get to know each other and to fall in love with each other. So they spend the day walking around talking, asking questions and eventually they sat down. The king explained to her that his desire is that both mankind and the animals reproduce and fill the earth, that he gave the earth and all that is in it, including the animals, to mankind. It was his gift to mankind. Now it was their responsibility to maintain and care for the earth.

Chapter 8

After waking up, King Raaph goes into the throne room. As usual the three leaders are there standing, waiting for the king to speak.

"Today is a new day in the kingdom. Today I will be showing you what I have been working on. All of the citizens shall know what I have been doing. Nemola, go now, take your team. Tell them to assemble the entire kingdom for a meeting this afternoon. Write this down Nemola: 'I hereby declare the king requests your presence in the courtyard just after lunch. Please come exactly at 12:30 and we will share the great news with you.' Go quickly and assemble your team."

So Nemola leaves the throne room and heads to the rest of his team members. They are all told the message and then they go to spread the news throughout the kingdom. Every citizen and every creature will be informed that they must join the king today. Nemola gives them the message and immediately they start to cover the entire kingdom giving the message to all.

"Raaph?"

"Yes, Lucarious?"

"So what is this news? Have you been working on something new? What is it my king?"

"Lucarious, you can wait and find out with the others."

"But king, shouldn't your trusted leaders know in advance? You seem so excited to tell us, so tell us."

"No, Lucarious, I think you can wait for the others who will all be informed together."

Lucarious just stands there staring at him. He is completely amazed; this must be the first time the king hasn't given him the news before everyone else. Lucarious feels funny that he won't know till everyone else. It must be important.

The time reaches 12:30 then Nemola flies back into the throne room and says, "Everyone has been informed and now everyone has been accounted for. You may proceed my king."

King Raaph heads out of the throne room and onto the balcony that overlooks the courtyard. The entire courtyard is full. He thinks to himself, "If I made one more citizen I would have to expand this courtyard."

"Hello, my fellow citizens. Thank you for stopping your busy day and coming to hear me. I have exciting news. I am so proud of all of you. I couldn't be happier, you make me feel like a good king and now I decided to show you what I have been working on.

Chapter 8

"First, Lucarious, I have good news. Your worship will look a lot different. Things are going to change in the kingdom, things will look much different. Lucarious, don't you think it's time for a change?"

"Yes, my king, I do think it's time for a change, it's about time that you finally changed your mind."

"Changed my mind? Changed my mind? What are you talking about Lucarious?"

"Well, king, you don't have to beat around the bush any longer, you called everyone here for a reason, correct?"

"Yes, Lucarious, that is correct."

"Well go ahead and tell everyone why worship will look different and how you finally decided to let me take a break and sit on your throne. It's about time I receive the honor I deserve."

"Lucarious, you think this is what this meeting is about, you think it's all about you? Well, my friend, I told you before that no creature that is created can ever be worshipped. You can never sit on my throne. Hahhahahhahaha."

The entire kingdom starts to laugh. Lucarious is totally embarrassed and his face turns red. He stands there and takes it. There is nothing he can do. He dare not leave in the middle of the king's meeting.

"No, Lucarious, I have decided to create again. Let me show you."

He snaps his fingers and the entire kingdom goes dark. He then points to a huge wall on the side of one of the buildings inside the court room. It suddenly turns into a movie projector screen. The projector starts and they watch and see that the king and his family have been leaving the kingdom in the evenings of the last few days. They suddenly realize they didn't even notice. Then they see the king creating a garden. They also see the earth filling up with new creatures they have never seen before. They see the clay doll and how the king blows air into his mouth and they see the clay doll come alive. They see the king walking and talking with him. They see the king teaching him how to do things. Next they see the king introducing another doll to earth. They see the king eating with the new creature and then knocking him out and removing his rib. They also see that this doll is being turned into another creature. This is unlike anything they ever saw before. This creature's face and figure is nothing like they have ever seen, except in their queen. No one else has ever looked like this before. They are all intrigued and excited, wondering if the king would ever give them a companion.

The movie ends and the king speaks to the light, "Light, come back," and suddenly the light is there again and the movie projector seems to disappear. They are all silent, not sure what to do or say next.

The king steps forward and says in a loud voice, "I have created a new creation. This creation I call man. Man will walk the earth and I created a garden for him to live in. There is no need for him to ever leave the garden. It will take him a long time to fill the garden for I have given him creative power. He will recreate

Chapter 8

himself with his companion. They will love each other and recreate and some day they will populate the entire earth. During this time they will be growing the garden. They will grow it into a huge world."

"But that's not why I assembled you here. I have brought you all here to tell you that I will be giving some of you new jobs. I will have the worship team go to the earth and worship me from there. They will fill all of the universes with their music. When I created all the universes, I purposefully created perfect acoustics. The sound will bounce off each universe perfectly until it reaches the kingdom. So everything now will hear the wonderful sound of our beautiful worship team. Next, the messenger citizens will be spending a lot of time in flight. They will go to the earth and deliver messages when needed. I personally will be visiting the earth every evening and I will be walking and talking with the new creation. I also will use the warrior citizens when needed on the earth."

Jira takes his wife's hand and continues to walk around the garden. He couldn't be happier with the partner that the king has given to him. "The king must know what he is doing," Jira says out loud.

Tamum says, "Why do you say that?"

"Because he gave me you, and I am enjoying everything about you. Well, it's close to evening and the king will be here very soon. He always shows up at this exact spot."

They walk over to the spot. So thinking that the sun seems to be where it usually is, they sit down

The Chosen One

on a rock and wait for the arrival of the king. King Raaph and his entire family show up. When they arrive everyone is so happy to see each other. They start to walk around the garden and talk.

"Jira, you know that you are going to have to teach her how to maintain the garden. You will need to bring her up to speed. You two will need to learn how to cook."

"What is cook?" asks Tamum.

"Well, my child, it is when you take the food that you have gathered that day and place it over the fire. You will change the taste and you will add different foods together to make different kinds of food. Be creative! I gave you a creative mind and you will be able to figure things out. Don't worry, I will be with you and I can talk to you and give you advice. It will be fun to learn together. Jira, walk with me."

So Kadesha and their son stay behind and Jira and the king walk away.

"Jira, I need you to understand that although you were first and you are the strong one and although I am leaving you in charge, you must consider your wife. Her opinion matters to me and it should to you. Do not underestimate the knowledge that she will have. She was created to be your equal so always love her, honor her and consider all that she says. All wise men from here on out will consider what their wives have to say. They will have great wisdom and also have a different thought process. They should

Chapter 8

never be ignored or put down. They are important to you. So love and cherish this gift I gave to you."

Jira was too busy listening to realize they just walked in a big circle and now they are back where they started from.

"It is now time for us to leave you. When you wake up, check on the plants and animals. Take care of your wife; continue to work on building her a more comfortable place to live and a comfortable place to sleep. I will see both of you tomorrow."

The next day Jira wakes up and stares at his wife, smiling and extremely happy with the partner that the king has given him. As she awakes she catches him staring at her and watching her. She wakes up with a smile on her face.

She asks him, "What are you doing?"

"Oh, me? Ah, nothing, just waiting for you to wake up. Come on and let's eat so we can get our work done." They both stand up and walk around the garden picking out the fruit they will eat.

They eat breakfast and after working all day, Jira says to his wife, "The sun is close to the spot in the sky where the king comes and visits us. We must hurry to the middle of the garden to greet him."

They finish up and walk to where their king usually comes. The king and his family show up at the meeting place. The king begins to teach them both many things. He shows them how to tell time by looking at the position of the sun. He shows them how to take the clay from the river bed to form bowls

The Chosen One

and cups. He teaches them that the sun will dry it up and strengthen it. He starts to walk around and talk to them about the fruit. He shows them how each fruit is different and does different things to their bodies. He teaches them about the importance of eating different fruit. He explains to them that everything, including the earth, needs and wants to be near to him; that if he stayed away from the earth for an extended period of time, the earth would start to rebel against man. They must never let that day come. So the king assembles his family and heads them to the middle where they leave. They all say their goodbyes and he reminds them to watch for him tomorrow. Then Jira and his wife walk to the back part of the garden where their home is located.Every day the king and his family come at the same time. Every day the king teaches them something new. He loves teaching them how things work. They now have shelter, bowls, cups and plates. He taught them how to cook and make many different kinds of food. Everything is going great. But the king and his family aren't all about work. They love to play and have fun. They all head to a wide and deep area of the river that is in the garden. They all enjoy walking in the water especially on the hot days. They love it, so cool and refreshing. It also helps them get refreshed. They love when the animals join them in the river and have fun splashing and getting each other wet. The king decides it's time to teach them about traveling. If they want to get from one end of the garden to the other very quickly,

Chapter 8

the animals can assist them in that. The king teaches them about riding the back of the horses as well. He teaches them that some animals are very strong and can push and pull heavy objects. Each night after teaching them something, the king and his family head back home.

Of course now that the kingdom citizens all know about his earthly children, they all want to know what happened every night. Every one of them is so full of curiosity. They can't help themselves. So after them asking so many questions every day, the king decides to hold nightly meetings with the entire kingdom. He shows them a movie on the side of a building every night. The movie is always what the king and his family did on earth that day. Everyone is curious about each other, they can hardly stand it. In each place, both dream of what it must be like to be on the other side of the kingdom.

Another day passes and the king and his family return. The family decides that they want to play today so the king being the biggest shows them how he takes his son and grabs his arms and locks them tight. He then starts to spin them around and around, until they both fall down dizzy. The son tries to stand up and falls right back down. Every one laughs and laughs and laughs. No one can wait, they all start asking to be next. Things similar happen every day and they just love spending every second with the king. The king also enjoys his time with his children. He loves each of them. This time before leaving, he tells them he will not be coming in the afternoon. They all look sad and disappointed. They can't believe it. They never had a day without the king before.

"Why, my king, why won't you come and visit us tomorrow."

"Oh, Tamum, don't worry I am coming tomorrow and I will be teaching you, but I will wait till later than usual to come."

So the next day, Jira and Tamum go on their normal day and gather the fruit and eat. They look after each animal and then head toward the river. They inspect everything and everyone down there. They are getting quite a routine down. Some days they check the rivers and other days the trees in the garden. Other days are for the animals. And other days they tend to their home and always lastly they tend to each other. It seems like it took the night time forever to come this time. It was such a long day without the king in the evening. Then they notice it getting darker. They walked the middle of the garden where they always met the king and they waited and waited. Just as they thought their king forgot about them, the king and his family gently fall to the earth.

"So how was your day?" the king asked.

"It was perfect my King, how was your day?"

The king laughs and says, "Everyday is perfect in my kingdom. So I decided to come late tonight. Let's walk over here just a little bit."

Chapter 8

They find a nice clearing in the fields. They lie down together and stare at the sky. The king starts to name many of the stars. He tells them a story about each one. He gives them the name and makes them repeat it after him. Then he tells them a story about it. After all of that, he tells them why he created it and the importance it has on the entire universe. He explains to them and they completely understand everything he is saying. After a long time, the king can tell that everyone is tired. So he starts to wrap it up for the night.

"Well, my children, I will come back the next few nights until I have taught you about every star."

Now that they understand the stars, the moon, the sun, and the many universes, he decides that he is going to teach them about the earth. There is so much that they will need to know. So that evening he sits them all down and explains to his wife, son and two earthly children how he created the earth.

He explains how he decided to create each system and how they all work together to keep their bodies going. He explains each part of all their internal systems. He explains many other things, also. He explains to them what is in the middle of the earth and how and why he had to do what he had to do. He explains there are mountains placed in the correct parts of the earth. They are created to let the steam out of the center of the earth so the center can breathe and continue to do what it does. This all works together to create an environment where plants can grow, water can be produced and these will support all of the animals and the children. They now completely understand how everything works together to keep everything alive, each system complementing other systems.

But all is not learning. The king and his family also come to the earth to eat with them once a week. They love to bring treats that aren't found on the earth yet. He will teach them how to cook more things as time goes by. The king and his family enjoy the days. They enjoy visiting the earthly children. Their favorite day is when they play games such as run around and spin around and land on the ground dizzy. Since the king is much larger than the rest of them, he is always picked to swing them. He locks their arms and starts to spin them like they were nothing more than a rag doll. They love this the most. Then they play a game to see who can walk the farthest without falling to the ground. Kadesha loves watching her husband interacting with their earthly children. So much for them to learn, so little time, she thinks to herself. She can feel the tension in the air when she walks down the streets of the kingdom. She knows the rebellion can't be far off. Her intuition is kicking into overdrive.

Chapter 9

The worship team finishes the last song of the day. Since the song is over, the bustle of everyone putting away their instruments can be heard, and the chairs moving around as they are gathering their things and the instruments cases. As they are putting their instruments away they hear Lucarious tapping his baton on the music stand. They all look up at him while they are continuing to put away their stuff. Lucarious looks each one of them in the eye and then nods. They know from previous meetings that he is calling another meeting. They know that they should all head to the cave at the normal meeting time just after dusk.

When dusk arrives, each member walks into the cave where there are torches already lit and hanging on the walls. They walk down the path that is lit up for them. After a few short minutes of walking, they come into a natural opening in the cave. There Lucarious is sitting and waiting. He is waiting for the entire group to arrive. Once they see that everyone has arrived, Lucarious stands up and starts to speak.

"As you all know, we are the best that King Raaph has. We all know that he can't live without his music. He must have us. So we need to stand up to him and give him our demands and he has to give in. Do you really think that he could endure silence in the kingdom? Silence hasn't been heard in the kingdom in many, many years. There is no way he could stand it. So I decided that since I am your leader, I must go to the king and demand things for you. He must allow us to go back to the kingdom. He must allow us to choose who can sit on the throne. We must be treated better. He needs us. So we have the upper hand. We can use it. I have listed all the rotten things he has done to us. We didn't do anything wrong. We don't deserve this. We shall go and demand he give us our place back in the kingdom. I do not want to be here on earth any longer. Every second I see that child of his, it makes me sick. I can't stand it nor can I stand him. Why did King Raaph give him so much? What makes him so special? Why did he get things we didn't? Do you realize he looks just like him? Did you know that first of all he created them with his own life force? Did you know that he gave them creative power? Did you know he made him ruler? Did you know that he gave him a mate? A help mate he calls it.

"Who is this Jira and what makes him so special? Why, why, why? I don't get it! I don't understand! What makes this creature so special? So special that he gets thing that you don't. Booka?"

"Yes, Lucarious."

Chapter 9

"Booka stand up." Booka stands up. "Booka, do you look like Raaph?"

"No, no I don't."

"Landalin stand up. Landalin do you have Raaph's life force inside of you?"

"NO, Lucarious, no, I don't."

"Neesha stand up. Do you have a help mate, someone to lie down with and keep you warm? Do you have someone to walk with and talk with all day long? One that was created specifically for you?"

"No, Lucarious, no, I don't."

"Zansibar stand up. Zansibar, were you given an entire planet to be ruler over?"

"No, Lucarious, I wasn't."

"See my friends, see? These citizens that are standing here in front of you make up all of us. We have been treated unfairly and unjustly. We never did anything wrong, we only did what the king asked us to. And what did we get for doing what he asked? We got banished, banished to this forsaken planet. This place is nothing like the kingdom. I'm not sure if I will ever understand why he made us come here. But we listened, didn't we?"

They all agree loudly.

"Yeah!" someone in the back yells. "We deserve better!" someone else yells, until the entire place fills with murmurs. Zansibar fears that this outburst will enrage their leader, but it doesn't seem to faze him at all.

Lucarious lets them go for a few minutes thinking to himself, "This is exactly what I need. I need them to be wound up."

After the shouting and complaining seems to die down, Lucarious jumps up onto a rock.

He says, "Fellow citizens, you have seen that I am like him. You have seen my creative power. You have seen I haven't done anything to harm you. You have seen I have done nothing to hurt you. You have seen that I only want the best for you. The best for you isn't what you have now. Now what you have is different. It's less than what you used to have. I want to restore you to what you used to have and make it better. I want to compensate you for all that you have lost. I want to compensate you for all that you gave up. And I want to compensate you for all that you never received. You will have a better life if you allow me to be your leader and not Raaph. First we must all make a pact. We must stand together. We will not be conquered. If he says no, then we must be prepared to fight for what is ours, for what we deserve. We can't come back to what we have, it's not an option. It's unconceivable! It's not acceptable! It won't happen! Now are you ready to go and demand what we want?"

"YAH!"

"Are you ready to go and get what we deserve?"

"YAH!!"

"Are you ready to do whatever it takes?!?"

"YAH!!!"

"Are you ready to fight for your rights?"

Chapter 9

"YAH!!! YAH!!!" The entire cave is filled with shouts and excitement.

After everyone leaves, Zansibar goes up to Lucarious and says, "You are a natural leader. They will follow you and they will obey your every command."

"Yes, Zansibar, I believe that they will follow me and they will go where I go and they will do what I say and they will be greatly rewarded for their loyalty."

"Lucarious, have you thought about what might happen if he says no again?"

"No again? No again?!? What's wrong with you? Don't be a fool! He can't say no again."

"But Lucarious, he has in the past. He told you no twice."

"He may have told me no, but I didn't have the support I have now. I didn't have the strength behind me. He told me no, but do you really think that he will tell all of them no? It's a huge part of his kingdom. And we all know how much he hates silence."

"Well, I don't know if he hates silence, that is pretty strong, but I do know that he loves to be worshiped."

"Zansibar, are you turning on me? I thought you were my go to guy. Can I not trust you anymore?"

"Oh come on, Lucarious, you know there is no one who is more loyal than me. Don't start with that garbage again."

"Well, are you going soft on me?"

"No, no I'm not."

"Ok, just curious. What's wrong with you?"

"Nothing's wrong, I just want you to consider all things. All things need to be considered. What you are proposing is no small thing, nor will the king take it as a small thing. He won't like it one bit."

"Small thing? I don't consider this as a small thing! I've been waiting for this moment for a long, long time. I've been dreaming of this moment for a long, long time. I can't wait for this moment. And it's just around the corner. It will be here soon enough. Besides if you are right and he says no, well then we will have to pressure him with a little force."

"Lucarious, you do realize that there are more of them than there are of us."

"Yes, but we are better and have more to offer. We are the worship team, aren't we? The messenger team and warrior team can't be his band. It would take years for him to create, raise and teach a new group all that we know. Quit worrying."

Lucarious and his team go each day and play the worship songs on earth as they were requested to by the king.

Everything seems normal from the outside looking in. The problem lies with inside of Kadesha who feels uneasy most of the time. She is having a hard time getting an entire night's sleep. She is tossing and turning a lot. She loves her husband and her king but knows that his best friend doesn't love him anymore. She wonders if there is any chance that the rebellion she feels coming would be wide spread. She knows inside that she is going to be surprised

Chapter 9

how many are deceived. She keeps dropping hints to her husband. He just doesn't seem to be getting it, why is he not concerned?

"Raaph, oh Raaph, where are you?" Kadesha walks around the palace looking for her husband. She finally walks into a room that they call their study. It's a large room with beautiful wooden walls and shelves and shelves of books. "Raaph!"

"Hum. Oh, yes, my dear."

"Raaph, I need to talk to you."

"Sure come in, what's on your mind my dear?"

"It's about the rebellion. I feel that it is growing. I feel that it is bigger than I first feared."

"Please my dear, there is nothing to fear. We should never fear. There is no room in this kingdom for fear. I know that we don't want anything like that around. Besides my dear, you are the one who is pure. If you are pure then you have no fear."

"Ok, well maybe fear wasn't the word I was looking for, but I am concerned about you, the rebellion, and how you will take it. What effect it will have on you and how it will be received inside the entire kingdom? Besides, every time I bring it up you don't want to talk about it or do anything with the information I bring you."

"Ok, let's talk about it. I didn't intend to make you feel like I didn't care about your feelings; I just don't want to waste my time thinking about it."

"Ok fine, but we need to talk about it now. Let's go ahead and waste a few minutes of our time."

"Ok, what do you want to talk about my dear? My time is yours, so tell me."

"Well, first, this is your best friend. He is also created by you and is lying about you and stealing your friends away, he is threatening to destroy you and take over. He wants to kill you and you haven't said a word."

"Aaaahhhhhh," the king takes a deep breath. "Well, my dear, this is how I feel. What's done is done and I refuse to do anything about it. I tried and tried to change his mind. I gave him everything he wanted. He was the best of the best and the most beautiful. I gave him responsibilities. He had the love and admiration of all the citizens, including my family. He had everything he ever wanted and he could have had more. There isn't anything I wouldn't have given him. So what does he do? He asks for the only thing I can't give him, the ability to be worshiped by all. No created being can be worshipped. It's not possible. It's not at all possible. Now that is what he wants and now he is going to try to take it by force. First, if I give it to him, it would cause mass destruction. It would cause an uprising among everyone. Things won't be as they are to be. I refuse to hand it over. After many attempts at changing his mind, I started to warn him and warn him and warn him. He still didn't listen, so at that point I decided to allow him to do whatever he wants. I don't want to force anyone to love me, you or our son. I don't want to force the citizens to love each other. I want it to happen naturally or it isn't true

Chapter 9

love, its forced love. Forced love is no different from slavery. So if we truly love him we must allow him to make up his own mind. We must love him enough to allow him to make his own decisions."

"Alright, I can agree and understand all that you have said. But why allow him to take more with him? They are yours, they belong to you and they also are your friends."

"Again my dear if I love them, I must love them enough to allow them to make their own decision. They must make up their own minds."

"What happens if they decide to fight?"

"It's not if my love, it's when, they have already decided in their hearts they will fight me if they have to fight me."

"Are you going to stand back and take it? Is that what you are going to do?"

"No, my dear, although love can cover over much, there are consequences to all of our actions. He will pay a large penalty for what he is about to do."

"Then what? Are you going to forgive and forget after the penalty?"

"No, my dear. I wish the answer were yes, but it will be no. After the penalty he will be so consumed with the penalty he won't try to change. He will grow worse, and with time he will grow stronger. He will become so full of himself and so full of hatred he will try to keep on hurting me or paying me back. He will go after the ones I love, then and only then when he touches my family will it be over for him."

"Touches your family? Touches your family? What do you mean; you think he is going after me or worse our son?"

"No, my dear, he will go after our earthly children. Then when he goes after them, his penalty will be an unbearable penalty—one that will last forever. He will pay highly for his actions."

"So now he is going to hurt Jira."

"No, he won't hurt them; he will try to get me to destroy them. They too will have to pay a penalty for their actions. But I love them; and since I love them they must make up their own minds."

"So then what, what will happen to them?"

"They will have to be saved from the mess they create."

"But who can save them?"

"Only one can save them, only one can change the situation. Only one can restore them back; that would be one who is perfect and one who would never go against me or turn his back—one whom I could trust with the entire kingdom. If this person proves themselves trustworthy, then and only then would they be worthy of being handed the entire kingdom.

"Well, there are only three people that fit that description. You, me, and our son."

"Yes, my dear, you are correct."

"Well you and I aren't going; nor would I want my son to be the one fix their mess."

"But Kadesha, don't you see that he is the one? He is it, he will be the deliverer, he will bring me my

Chapter 9

children back to their created state and then they can come and live with us forever."

"You want our son to do it?"

"Yes, my dear, I want my son, our son, to be the one who is worthy of our kingdom, I want to give my son everything he wants and more. I want to give my kingdom to my son."

"So how will it happen? How will our son be the one to save our children from themselves?"

"He must live a pure life, one that has never been lived before. He will pay the penalty that he doesn't owe. Then he can pick and choose how to run the kingdom. He will be able to make the decisions as it will be his kingdom."

"It doesn't sound easy."

"You are right; it isn't going to be easy. I will have to pour out all of my hatred of disobedience on him. Then he will be the reason that every earthly child will be forgiven."

"How will that happen?"

"It's easy; they will just have to ask for it. That simple. They will just have to be sorry for what they did and then ask and since he already paid the price we can always say yes and will always say yes."

"Just that simple?" Kadesha asks.

"Yes, my dear, just that simple. I want it to be simple since they were lied to. They can be forgiven, but I'm not going to allow them to pretend they weren't part of it either. They willingly disobeyed, so there will be penalties for them. I'm not going

The Chosen One

to make it easy on them. They won't be able to just blame him for their actions. They must confess that they were an active participant."

"Well, it's not going to be easy watching our son pay for everyone's mistakes."

"I know it's not going to be at all. I don't want him to leave for any amount of time. That won't be easy either." *Ccccrrasssshh.*

They both stop and look over at the crash that just happened. They both see their son hiding behind an end table. The both look at each other and realize it's too late; he had to have heard everything.

"Come here son," says the king. He quietly walks over to his father. He doesn't know what to think, he is scared because he was never in trouble before. There wasn't much for him to get into trouble about.

So he walks to his father, his father says to him, "Have a seat, son."

His father slides a chair right in the middle of him and his mother. His mother grabs his hands and gently strokes them; his father places a hand on his knee and looks into his eye. "How much of that did you hear my son?'

"A lot," he says.

"Well, I need to know how much."

"I was walking down the hall and I heard your and mother's voices, so when I got closer to the door I was going to walk in and I heard you talking about a rebellion. I froze and listened. I didn't know what to think. So I slowly walked in the room. Neither of

Chapter 9

you saw me; so then you started to talk about me and that's when I sat down on the floor and just listened. I wasn't trying to make you mad father, honest."

"I know, my son, and I'm not mad. We need to talk about this anyway my son. I just didn't want it to be this way."

"Well, father I don't mind, I really want to help. I want to help you and mother and Jira. You are all my family."

"It's ok, son, it will be alright. So here it is. Lucarious is upset and he will start a fight with me. Since he cannot hurt me, he will attack the things I love and from there we are going to need you. You will be the hero in this story. How does that sound? Do you want to be a hero?"

"Well of course, father, but were you being honest when you said you wanted to give me your kingdom?"

"Yes, why do you ask?"

"Well it's your kingdom and you're the one who created all of this."

"Yes, that is true, go on."

"Well why would you give it to me?"

"Son, there isn't anything any good father wouldn't give to his children. Fathers were designed to want to give their children all that they can. That is the way they were made."

"Why is that?"

"Well that's how much I love you. I want you to have it all. So I designed my earthly children to respond the same way. So how do you feel about going to earth and living as an earthly child?"

"Really? You mean I can be born as an earthly child?"

"Yes, that is what I am planning on doing with you, allowing you to be born. You can go and live a clean life and then everyone who didn't live a clean life can be brought back into the family because of you. How does that sound?"

"It sounds great father. I can't wait, when can I go?"

"Slow down my son, it hasn't happened yet."

"But father I don't know if you know this, but every citizen wants to know what it's like to be an earthly child. They all want to go and become a child and see what it's like. They all are going to be excited for me when I go. Then I can come back and tell them. I want to go. I must go for me and them."

"Ok, ok, slow down; it won't be for awhile yet. But you must not tell anyone about this conversation or my conversation to your mother. They must not know what is happening. It could change the outcome. You just be prepared, on alert and on guard for something like the kingdom has never seen before."

"Ok, father, I won't."

Chapter 10

"Good morning, Lucarious, long time no see."
"Nemola, Kanamoola, what are you two doing here? Please tell me that Raaph hasn't sent you to live here also. I'm not enjoying my stay here. I'd much rather be walking around in the kingdom."

"Well, Lucarious, the answer is sort of."

Nemola and Kanamoola look around and see Lucarious' team tuning up and getting ready. It was about that time. In just a few moments the team would start to play and the entire universe would hear the music.

"Well, Lucarious, King Raaph has decided that we are going to spend time on earth."

"For what reason would you two ever need to come here? He used some lame excuse about the acoustics and sound travel and bounce to force me to come to this terrible place. What is his excuse, why could he possibly think it was a good idea to send you two here?"

"Well, Lucarious," Nemola chimes in, "Kana is here to protect the earthly children. He is now their guardian. I, as you know, am the messenger. I will be bringing messages from the king to you, Kana, and his children. That way if his earthly children decided they wanted to talk to the king, they can tell me and I will be the one to deliver the message."

"Are you kidding me? Please tell me you are joking."

"No, Lucarious. Why wouldn't we be truthful with you? Why do you ask these questions?"

"Ask these questions? Ask these questions? Why aren't you standing up for yourself? Why aren't you challenging him and having him see it your way? What's wrong with you two?"

"What's wrong with us? What's wrong with you Lucarious? How can you speak this way? The king won't like it one bit. He will be very angry when he finds out how you are talking."

"Wait a minute, Nemola, don't you see what he is doing? Can't you see that we are now nothing and these stupid kids of his are everything? We suddenly aren't anything anymore."

"Why are you talking like this? Please, Lucarious, please stop before you get in to more trouble than you are going to be."

"Going to be? What, are you going to go and tell on me?"

"Of course, I am a messenger and I must deliver all the messages. Beside he already knows. So there is no way I can't, you know that. I mean come on, really Lucarious. What's gotten into you lately?

Chapter 10

What's the problem with you lately? You haven't been yourself for a long time and don't tell me it's because you don't like earth. It started way before that. We can tell."

"Let me just tell you what's wrong. He sent you, Kana, and me here to follow around some snot nosed kid he calls child. We are his best, we are all he has; and he sends us. He sends us to come to the earth to serve his children. They aren't anything like us. They are worthless. Just look at them! They can't do anything but yet he gave them more than he gave us. Can they fly, can they travel back and forth from the kingdom by themselves, and can they stand in the throne room? No! So why then did he give them a helper, why did he give them the earth to rule, why did he give them creative power? Nemola, do you have creative power?"

"No, Lucarious."

"Kana, do you have a help mate?"

"No, Lucarious."

"Exactly! He gave them much more than he gave you and me. They aren't even up to our height let alone our standards. And now, and now we are going to follow around a bunch of children who are worthless, should we wipe their noses for them too?"

"Lucarious, stop!"

"No, you stop. I'm not done, listen up. I can't take it anymore. Listen to me, your awesome and mightly, all loving, all caring King Raaph used his own life force and his own air from his own lungs to create this so called child of his."

Kana and Nemola can hardly believe their ears. "Every one of the citizens loves the king and wants to be just like the king. Everyone cares so deeply for the one who is responsible for creating them. They all want to be like him. Better yet, they all want to be him. They always knew the life force is what separated them from their king."

"Lucarious, you are making that up!"

"No, Kana, I'm not. I read the manuals in his shed. Day by day I would sneak in there and read and read and read. I discovered a long time ago that he was going to use his life force as their basic building block. I got mad and that is when you guys say that I changed. I say that's when I got smarter. If he could do that, then he could give me what I want. He could give you want you want. Did you two want to live down here and be here bored to tears, following some silly child around so he doesn't fall out of the tree and get hurt?"

"No, Lucarious, we didn't."

"So then forget the message, let's go and talk to him. Let's go and tell him how we feel, let's go get what we want. Let's go tell him we won't serve his children. Let's tell him we aren't servants."

"Lucarious, you make many good points but I am going to listen to the king. I will choose to serve him and follow his lead."

Chapter 10

"Of course you would Kana, you're his brainwashed warrior citizen, head of all his brainwashed citizens."

"Nemola, come on, let's go."

"No, Lucarious, I am going to stay here. I am going to follow my king and when he calls me I will return to the kingdom."

By this time Lucarious turns around and realizes that the music should have started by now and that everyone on his team has quietly walked up behind him and listened to every word.

"Nemola and Kana, you have been my friends forever. I have loved you two more than I loved anyone else. Please think about what you are saying, what you are doing, and what you are subjecting yourself to. Servanthood. You are going to now and forever serve a child that is meaningless. Come, let's talk to Raaph and tell him."

"Lucarious, we are sorry but you have already overstepped your boundaries. There is no turning back. The king already knows what we are talking about and we will not allow this to go any farther, nor will we get into trouble because of your mouth and attitude. We won't allow it."

"Listen up you two, I don't need you! I don't need any of you. I will never bow down and serve this silly little creature. Just look at him. I am down here allowing him to hear my music. I am done. I had enough and I am going to tell Raaph I'm done. In fact I will head up to the kingdom. I will go into the palace. I will head into the throne room and I will force him to give me what I want. I will force him to hand over his throne. I will force him to allow me to be a ruler. I will be the one to get the worship and I will be like him. No, better yet I will be him."

Kana yells, "Lucarious, how do you suppose you are going to do this? You know he will never give in to those ideas."

"By force, my friend, by force."

"You think you can take away his throne?"

"No, my team and I will take away his throne and I will become him."

Kana looks over at Nemola who knows that he is the fastest, shakes his head and nods towards the kingdom. Lucarious' eyes get huge. He realizes for the first time he will have a fight on his hands. He never considered that the other citizens would stick up for the king. He thought that they would just become spectators. Kana jumps and then takes off towards the kingdom, going faster than he ever flew before.

Lucarious turns and yells to his team. "Let's go! The time is now. Go to the kingdom and enter through the side door. There is a closet to the left; there I have already hidden many swords. Zansibar, go first and hand everyone a sword. Booka ,Landalin, and Neesha, you grab your smaller team and each take a corner of the throne room. Let me do the talking. Let me handle it if there is any resistance. Immediately go into fight mode. Don't wait for me, just start to

Chapter 10

fight. But no worries, he can't stop all of us. We will win without a fight. We can take it. Go now."

The entire team starts to run and jump and then fly straight up and into the kingdom. They all go and do what Lucarious says. He gets there first, grabs his sword and places it inside his belt loop. He walks in to the throne room where King Raaph is sitting on his throne. "Lucarious, what are you doing here?"

"I am here to tell you that the entire team has decided we will not give you any more worship and there will be silence in your kingdom forever."

"Oh, really?" says King Raaph.

"Unless you allow me to sit on the throne and be worshiped. Nor will we ever follow around your earthly children and serve them unless you allow me to sit on your throne. In fact if you want, you can even give me my own throne. Place it beside yours, King Raaph . What do you say?"

King Raaph is smiling and happy as always. He says. "Well, Lucarious, I hope you are joking."

"Joking? You better reconsider your words King Raaph because I'm not joking, nor will I ever joke around about such a serious matter."

"Serious matter? There is nothing serious about this, it is all quite absurd."

"Absurd? Absurd? You think that me having my own throne sitting beside you is absurd?"

"Yes, Lucarious, you sitting on the throne receiving worship is absurd. It won't happen. Not now, not ever."

Lucarious can't take it anymore. He can't take the king's happiness or his calmness. "Well, king, let's see how calm you are while you are outside looking in at me on my throne."

Kana says, "I've had enough" and he steps in front of the throne.

"It's ok, Kana, you can stay behind me. There is no reason for force."

Lucarious keeps stepping closer and closer to the throne.

"Lucarious, your answer is no and will always be no. Now please go back to earth and start up the band which is late. Let's get back to your jobs. Serving my earthly children isn't a hard job, nor is it below you. Just please go back and do your job."

Lucarious is completely red by now. "I can't take it anymore. Get off my throne or be killed."

As soon as he says that, Kana steps forward again and raises his sword.

"Kana, get back!" the king starts to say.

But it's too late. Lucarious' entire team takes it as a threat and they all rip out their swords; raise them and start running forward, yelling at the top of their lungs. The king turns and realizes it's too late. He can't get Kana to step back and even if he could, it's too late.

King Raaph jumps top his feet and yells, "SILENCE!"

The sound is so deafening and so loud it just about brings the entire kingdom to its knees. For the first

Chapter 10

time in history, since the beginning of creation, there is one hundred percent total silence. He looks back and motions to Nemola to remove his wife and son. Everyone's eyes are on his wife and son; they watch them leave. When he is sure they are far enough away from it all, he begins.

"Once and once only. You maybe be completely forgiven and totally restored for what you have done and what you are about to do. I will forgive all and forget all with one exception. And that exception is you, Lucarious, so if anyone else realizes that you have gone too far and wants to change their mind, I highly recommend you lay down your sword and walk out of the room. Do it now." Many of the team members feel that they want to go back to the way things used to be. Many want to stay with the king and live in his kingdom. But they are so afraid; they all stand frozen in time.

After a few seconds, Lucarious says, "See king, you are outnumbered. They will help me take my rightful place. They will..."

"Silence...once again...if you want to leave do it now."

The entire room fully realizes this is the first time they have ever seen the king without a smile. He had never looked this way to them before.

"Lucarious, I have given everyone a second chance and just to be sure a third chance. I would give them more; but I know that you have turned their hearts against me, so there is no use wasting my breath.

"You will forgive all of them," Lucarious says in a snide, smart way.

"All but you. I will not give you a second chance because everyone in this room has been lied to. Everyone has had you whispering lies into their ears. You have tickled their ears with nonsense. But not you. You have no one to blame but yourself. You changed and you didn't have anyone lying to you. So for that I will not forgive. Nor will I ever forgive. I can forgive someone who was lied to and believed it. Lucarious, you had it all, you could have had anything you wanted. You were my best friend. I gave you the most possessions. I gave you the most of my time. I allowed you to have the love and admiration of the other citizens. I gave you the most responsibilities. I gave you everything I had to give you. What were two things that I reserved for myself that you couldn't have? One was my wife. You can't ever, nor will you ever have her. The second thing that I reserved for myself was my throne. You can not, nor will you ever be allowed to be worshiped by my kingdom or anything in it. Never. Was that too much to ask for, you were supposed to be my best friend? Was that too much to ask for? Was it?"

There was a long pause, so long that you heard his words "was it" echoing for what seemed forever. It seemed to bounce off everything that was ever created in all the universes.

Chapter 10

After the long silence the king resumes, "All you ever wanted was to be a creator and have a title that showed you are a creator. So now I will bestow upon you everything you ever wanted. Now and forever you will be known as the creator of lies. I now take away your name Lucarious, no longer will you be known as Lucarious, but you will be known as "the father of lies."

The king starts to turn his back from everyone and walk towards his throne. He gets about half way from his throne and he hears Lucarious yelling back at him.

"Do you really think you can make it one day without worship? Worship is what you live for, isn't it? Isn't that the reason you created all of us? Isn't it? You are so greedy that you created an entire race just so that you could have people bowing down to you and around you. You created so someone would walk around thinking you were so great. How could your greediness possibly live without worship? You can't do it, you know you can't."

"Lucarious, you fool. You think that I created worship for me?" He laughs and shakes his head. "Lucarious, I will allow you to know that I am perfect. I am perfection. Since I live in perfection I have a need for nothing. Nothing at all. I created worship for you and for them. He points towards the kingdom.

Lucarious says, "Really, that makes no sense. How could we possibley be the ones benefiting from worship? It's for you and all about you. It's all about you."

"Lucarious, first of all, worship was a gift from me to you. Again, I need nothing. Since I need nothing, I decided to create worship so that you could touch my heart. It was a gift for you. You had it all, Lucarious, you were in charge of leading all of creation into a place that for once I became vulnerable. I allowed myself to become so vulnerable that you are able to touch my heart."

Lucarious stands there in silence, not sure what to do or what to say with this new revelation. After standing there for a moment he thinks to himself, "Well it doesn't matter anymore because it's too late for me. I can't be forgiven."

King Raaph looks him in the eye the entire time. The king turns and walks toward his throne. He stops, turns and sits down.

"Now, now that you completely understand everything, realize this, that everything I have done was for every one of you; I never did anything but good for you."

Lucarious knows if the king keeps talking, he will change the hearts of the rebellion back to himself. The king already announced it, he can't be forgiven and he can't be expelled while the rest of the rebellion stays here without him. No way, he won't let that happen.

"You think you can sweet talk us with your words, well it won't happen. You are manipulating everything, just as you always have. You are perfect, you are a perfect manipulator."

Chapter 10

The king laughs. "That is the funniest thing I ever heard you say." The king, who is now sitting back on his throne, is once again smiling. That makes Lucarious furious.

He raises his sword and yells, "Attack!!!" Lucarious jumps up and starts to run towards the king with his sword out high in the air. King Raaph stops, turns, and points and looks to the walls where there the entire messenger citizens come out from hiding behind curtains and decorations along the walls of the throne room. Lucarious looks at what the king is pointing at and sees the messengers coming out of hiding.

Lucarious starts to laugh. "They are nothing, nothing!"

The messengers start to attack from the sides. The king smiles and points upward. The whole entire time the whole entire conversation was also heard and witnessed by every warrior citizen quietly awaiting his orders while flying up towards the ceiling of the throne room. No one bothered to look up, if they had, they would have seen the warriors hiding in plain sight. The warrior leaders yelled "Charge!" The warriors hit the rebellion from over their heads. They were ambushed from all around. Swords striking swords could be hear all over the kingdom.

Kadesha and her son watched from the balcony, which was far enough away that nothing could hurt them. The king continues to sit on his throne, smiling as always. The rebellion hit the messengers and started to get somewhere with the messenger citizens. They were what seemed to be winning. The rebellion kept striking blow after blow after blow. They worked hard and started to tire out the entire messenger team. Swing after swing after swing, their arms were tired from hitting their swords against other swords.

The warrior team only allowed a few of their team to get into the battle to help them out. After what seemed to be hours of a heated battle which seemed to go back and forth on who was winning and who was in control, the warriors could see the rebellion was tiring out a little and the messengers were also tiring out. The warriors decided to move in. This was it. They knew they were completely refreshed and the best trained that King Raaph had. They knew it was now or never. They didn't want to give anyone any chance or anyway to get anywhere near the king. That was not an option in their mind. They ran striking their swords against the other swords. They turned and twisted and hit and hit. It was an amazing sight to sit back and watch and see. It was unbelievable. The warriors seemed to strike the enemy and spin and turn almost like a dancer was dancing. They seemed to almost dance between their new enemies, the rebellion, and the messengers, whom they loved. They never once hit or hurt a messenger. The rebellion, on the other hand, had taken many strikes. Of course, Lucarious was the tallest and that gave him an advantage over the

Chapter 10

others. Lucarious' strikes were hard and fierce, as he had much more to lose than the others. He must not be defeated, especially in front of his friends. He struck sword after sword hitting harder and harder with each swing. He split a few battle axes in half during the struggle. He couldn't be seen as a loser in front of his new kingdom. He couldn't lose; he must win especially now that the current king embarrassed him in front of so many citizens. It just can't happen. He fought and struck many, knocking them down, then kicking them aside and on the smooth floor of the throne room—it was easy for the fallen ones to slide across the floor slamming into the walls at times. Pushing his way forward, he didn't dare turn back and look to see what was going on. He could not bear the thought that he may be the only one advancing his cause for his kingdom.

The other citizens knew what was going on because although it was lit up very brightly, the entire kingdom darkened. The movie projector turned on and everyone came running from every corner of the kingdom. No one could believe their ears, let alone their eyes. They all felt pain inside the chest for the first time ever. They hadn't experienced pain before. They were sad that their friends and neighbors would attempt such a thing—Lucarious was a celebrity to them and this surprised them the most. Although he was loved, none of them had any desire to join in or even sympathize with what he was doing and trying to pull. This was absurd in their mind. Why would anyone ever want to, let alone attempt to do it? It just didn't make any sense. They also started to feel a little bit of anger towards Lucarious; he had it all, he had what others thought was perfection, and plentiful. They definitely knew he had more than they did and they didn't feel jealous, or sad, or even mad. They felt happy for him and proud to be his friend. No one felt they wanted what he had. It just didn't make any sense.

Lucarious continues to work his way toward the king; the rebellion is now showing that it is weak and tired and running out of steam. As soon as some turn their heads behind them to make sure no one is doing a counter attack, they realize their friends are being captured slowly but surely one by one. This doesn't help their desire to continue. Slowly the warriors take a captive, disarm him and then one messenger holds him down. This takes them from two to one, to three to one, then four to one, and on and on. This allows more to move forward from the rear. Each time they capture one, this allows more to gang up on the rear one. Each time they capture one, it's a tired messenger's job to restrain him. Back at the front, Lucarious is down to having only Kana left. Kana is waiting, holding his sword up to his face. Each eye is looking straight at him. The edge of the sword is pointed towards Lucarious. Kana is standing before his king daring Lucarious to step forward and try to cross the line.

Lucarious stops and breathes. Kana notices that his eyes have changed. They are no longer the bright

Chapter 10

and brilliant color they once were; they are turning darker. Now his eyes make you feel like they pierce right through you. Lucarious lets his arms down and then stands there for a moment, breathing heavily. He rests, but only for a second. The adrenalin rushes to his brain and he feels strength again. He starts to walk towards Kana, every step piercing him with his eyes. Although most citizens, whether they were warriors or not, would have been intimidated from the stare, Kana was trained so well that nothing could become a distraction, nothing. Lucarious stops and turns around. He sees that although it is really hard to tell because the fighting is so fierce, battle axes swinging, swords swinging, citizens holding each other in holds, he feels pretty sure that this is his only chance. If he doesn't destroy Kana and remove the king from his seat and occupy the seat, then he is finished.

Lucarious underestimates his king and Kana. Lucarious had favor and favor always got him what he wanted. He learned at an early age that he was different and things happen differently for him than others. The same situation for him and another citizen and there were always two completely different outcomes. Lucarious looks up and sees the king still sitting on his throne. He also sees that he is still smiling.

"Why is he smiling, what is wrong with this king? There is a fight for his throne and his kingdom, and he sits there and smiles. Is he mad, has he gone crazy?"

Kana steps forward. Kana's hands are gripping the sword tightly, his hands held up to the right side of his lips. Slowly stepping forward and then to the side walking around like an animal circling his prey, his eyes are locked onto his opponent's eyes. Swords are being tilted in almost a false move to try to get the other to strike first. Lucarious starts to circle around and keep Kana far enough away. Lucarious knows that Kana is a warrior and that warriors have a code of honor. They are to be protectors. This would go on all day if he doesn't make the first move. Lucarious lets out a scream and runs towards Kana. As soon as he is close, he takes his sword and swings it from his right and forces it downward to the left in front of him, but as soon as it gets half way it comes to a complete stop. Kana's sword just met it in the middle. The vibration is loud and harsh; Lucarious can hardly believe how harsh the vibration was to his hand. He never expected that. Come to think of it he had no training with a sword, let alone training with the sword striking something. But it didn't matter, he told himself. He knew he had desire and zeal, he knew that nothing could get in the way of his desire to sit on that throne. He could only imagine the feeling of having the entire citizenship showing their love to you out loud and on purpose. He must fight, he must win. Lucarious continues to swing and strike, swing and strike. With each hit, it becomes harder and harder to hold on to the sword. But stopping and giving up isn't an option. He will stop Kana at all costs. Nothing can beat him, nothing will beat him. He will win. But he is breathing heavier and heavier

Chapter 10

by the second. Kana looks the same, still has the serious look and is still turning and circling his prey. He is not worn out; in fact after this fight, he's going to look for the next one. This is what he lives for; this is what he trained for.

Kana flashes back to remembering the king making him do pushups until he couldn't move, not only couldn't move, he was still extremely sore and could hardly get out of bed the next day. As a little kid this never made sense to him. It was so hard to watch and see the king sitting on the grass with him—telling him to push it, do more, keep it up and on and on and on it went. When he would collapse to the ground he would always look over and see his friend Lucarious standing on the balcony; he never had the same instrument in his hand. One day Lucarious would be playing the violin and the next day he had a guitar in his hand. But Kana got something no one else did. He got a completely different schedule. The king would push and push and push and work him till he thought he was going to die, and then he got two days off. For the next two days he could do whatever he wanted to do. He could come and go as he pleased. No one else could do that, so he used it to his advantage. Just when he thought he couldn't do one more push up he thought to himself; I get two days off. Then suddenly out of nowhere, there he was doing three more.

Kana flashes back as the vibration from the swords hitting together sends vibrations though his arms. Kana decides he's had enough, this isn't fun for him. Most warriors are having fun, this is what they have trained for, but not Kana, he is miserable. This is his older brother in his mind. Nemola and he looked up to Lucarious. He was whom they wanted to be, he was the reason they both pushed themselves so hard to obtain perfection.

"Who didn't look up to Lucarious? He had it all; he was the king's best friend. Why would he want to do such a thing? What possibly could give him the desire to do something like this? Raaph must be upset, hurt, and saddened, too."

Kana decided enough was enough. He struck Lucarious' sword and held it there. With every muscle he had in his body flexing with all they had, he kept pressure on Lucarious' sword. He kept it still and walked up sword to sword and got in Lucarious face and said, "Enough is enough, I was being nice, but I am done."

With that said, he pushed Lucarious' sword towards Lucarious, stepped back and swung his sword with all that was in him. He hit the sword with all that he had and it was so powerful that as Lucarious tried to hold on, the force knocked the sword behind him and since he refused to let go, the sword took him down with it. Kana walked over and stood with each leg straddled over Lucarious' chest. He slammed his sword into Lucarious' shirt just left of his chest. Kana reached down and picked up Lucarious sword and slammed it into the right

Chapter 10

of Lucarious shirt. Lucarious was pinned between the two swords. He could only lay there. Kana walked around and found that all of the rebellion was defeated. No one was left to fight. Not only that, no one had any fight left in him. Kana walked around and handed out straps. They strapped each member of the rebellions' hands together so that they couldn't use them. They lined them up and made them stand before the king.

King Raaph stands up and walks through the crowd. He doesn't say a word. He finally gets to the end; none of the rebellion would look him in the eye. Finally he made his way from the back up to the front.

He stands and places his foot on Lucarious' chest and says, "I defeated you and I didn't even have to do a thing. Did you really think that you could defeat me, did you really thing that you were so great, so powerful that one third of my closest friends could actually overthrow my kingdom by defeating an army twice your size? This wasn't even a struggle. I could have stopped it before it began today, but I wanted you to see that I would defeat you with more than my authority. I have power over you also."

He removes his foot and calls for his family. Nemola goes and gets them from the balcony and escorts them straight to the throne. They all are now seated.

"Kana, stand him up."

Kana removes one sword and places it back into his belt loop. He grabs Lucarious' shirt and picks him up and drops him. Lucarious quickly stands to his feet.

"Lucarious, my old best friend and now my foe, you didn't win nor will you ever win. I now command you and your team to never come back. Kana, I want you and your warrior team to hold these guys. Nemola, I want you to take your team and assemble to my right."

Kana's team grabs their hands and stand beside each rebellion team member. Quickly, Nemola's team follows the king's orders. They all are lined up standing in front of the king awaiting their orders. They all stand at attention.

"Nemola, I want you to take your team. I want each member to stand outside the garden and slam your swords into the ground as far as you can. Then hold on tight and keep the garden safe and still. I don't want Jira and Tamum to know what is happening. I want them to know nothing; I want them to feel nothing. I want them to have a normal day."

Immediately the entire team goes to the obsitorium and heads straight for earth. As they land, they pull out their swords. They slam their swords deeply into the earth as they systematically land one by one surrounding the garden. When the last reaches within a few feet behind Nemola, he knows the entire garden is circled so he yells, "Hold on!"

They look up and see a huge dark cloud over head. They are wondering what is next.

Chapter 10

Back in the kingdom, Raaph is telling Lucarious that he must pay for his actions.

"Lucarious you have done me wrong, for this I now release you to the earth. You cannot live in the kingdom for one more second and since there is no other place that I created that can sustain life, I must ban you to the earth. That feels appropriate anyway. Since you don't like it there, it's ironic that you have been banished to inhabit the earth. I will allow you to stay there. But before you will be expelled to earth, I want you to do one more thing for me."

King Raaph picks up a mirror that he brought with him. It's a mirror that was made for his wife to hold and look at herself at the same time. He walks around and places it in front of each one of their faces. He doesn't move until he sees that they have each looked into it.

"Members of the rebellion, I want you to take a good, long look at yourself. It's important that you remember what you look like. I want you to have it engrained in your head. I also want you to think about the mansion in which you used to live when you were a kingdom citizen. I now hereby revoke your citizenship. I also take away your house. It will be given to your enemies, and everything in it will become theirs. So please think what is in your house and the things you have in each room and in each drawer. It's gone from you forever; you will never see it or own it again. What you are about to face will not be easy or pleasant for you. I hope it was worth it to you because it wasn't worth it to me. Just remember you had it all and you gave it all away. You could have had anything you ever wanted or desired, but that isn't what you chose. No matter what, always remember it was what you chose and you chose it by yourself. Lucarious, I now command you to leave my kingdom, I command you to leave everything behind. I banish you to the earth. It will not be a nice life at all. It will never end. I was hoping you would not go through with this. I was hoping you would listen to my hints and advice. I was hoping that you could have changed your mind. Lucarious, I hear by pronounce you banished to the earth. You may not ever reside in the kingdom ever again. I revoke your citizenship and the citizenship of the entire rebellion. You may no longer come and go as you please. You may not take anything with you except your memories of this place. I hope that you can see how badly you messed up. Nothing will be taken with you, not even your beauty."

Warrior citizens remove the retaining braces. Each warrior citizen pulls out his sword. Each one of them starts to blow on their sword. The swords begin to glow red. With a short and fast swoop, each warrior then slices the retaining braces off the hands of the enemy. Each member of the rebellion starts to rub their wrists, each one bending and turning their wrists, each one liking the new freedom their hands feel.

King Raaph stands in front of each one of them and yells, "BE GONE!"

Chapter 10

With that, the power in his voice knocks each of the rebellion team members off their feet. They fly backwards, never hitting the ground. It's as if a sonic tidal wave has lifted them up off their feet and pushed them backwards. The wave continues to push them back towards the obsitorium and over the edge. Each member is falling fast toward the earth. Their bodies start to spiral round and round and round as they fall. The problem is that as they are falling, they are so concerned with falling that they don't realize their bodies are changing.

CHAPTER 11

Down on the earth, Nemola and his messenger citizens are holding onto their swords. Nemola looks up and yells, "It's time."

They look up and see that thing they thought was a black cloud was fast approaching them. They all realize it is getting closer. The hard part is all they know is that they are to hold onto their swords and keep the garden still. The wind starts to whip their hair around. It starts to blow things around them everywhere. They hold on tighter to their swords as they see and hear a loud crash. The crash was so hard and so loud that it shook the entire earth. They hold their swords and keep the garden completely still while the entire planet is going wild. The force of them falling is cracking the ground. It shakes the ground so hard it starts to split. As each rebellion team member hits the ground they roll one way or another, each hitting the ground hard and bouncing different ways. The ground splits and shifts again and again. The ocean waters come up in the middle of the cracks and each broken off piece of land is picked

Chapter 11

up and carried away from the garden. There are now five major pieces of land moving far away from the garden. Tidal waves are sweeping them far away. They float off breaking up the earth and demolishing pieces of land with it. Smaller chunks of land are falling away, too.

The force of the rebellion hitting the earth was so hard and so fierce the earth will never be the same. Huge land masses are picked up and swept way. The huge land masses are trying to float but can't control the water hitting them. The dinosaurs are knocked over and fall to the ground. The water is flooding the land masses at the same time. The huge animals struggle for survival but most are drowning in the waves. Their bodies lay dead on the land masses. They didn't have a chance to save their own lives. They move until the bottom catches on something underneath. The lands come to a quick halt when their bottoms hit something not seen under the ocean. The land masses stop and settle where ever they get caught up underneath. The water is still slamming around. It will take hours for it to calm down and quit slamming into the land masses as hard as it is. The water is cutting and shaping the masses to look so very different than they were created.

Meanwhile the entire messenger team is holding the garden completely still. Jira and Tamum don't have any idea that anything is happening. It all seems to be a normal day all around them. Many hours after the waters all calmed down, the entire rebellion regained consciousness and stood up. The earth looks much different to them from the last time they were there. Nothing seems the same at all. The first thing they notice is that the dinosaurs were all very still and no movement came from them at all. Why were they lifeless? Would the king allow the effects of the rebellion to change the earth forever? Was this even possible? Was it?

The rebellion saw new creatures and laughed at them. They were tiny, puny, and ugly. When they looked hard at the faces of these new creatures they decided that these creatures' faces resembled someone they knew—someone in their rebellion. They started to look at each other and they laughed. They saw these new creatures were tiny and ugly. Suddenly the words of King Raaph came rushing back into their heads. "You may not take anything with you, not even your beauty."

Suddenly struck with fear, they realize they had gone from being over ten foot tall to being one foot tall. Suddenly they are all tiny little creatures who have no power. When they try to move things around is when they realized their power and strength was gone. They were sick to their stomachs. Lucarious told them he had the power and the perfect plan to make the king share his seat. He wanted the seat and they wanted Lucarious' position. They wanted him out of the way so they could compete to be the next leader and receive all the admiration that comes with that job. Just playing an instrument and doing their

Chapter 11

job suddenly wasn't enough. So they joined together and decided to help Lucarious take what he wanted so they could gain what he had.

Lucarious was starting to come to, also. He felt every inch of his body aching. He hurt all over, it wasn't just a fall; he said to himself, it was a slam. He started to see that there were many, many tiny creatures walking around helping each other stand up. He noticed dead animals all around. They became lifeless beings. He realized that the earth had changed. It didn't look the same. Nothing was the same. Everything not only looked different, but felt different. He felt so plain. He felt like he was weaker. The weirdest thing is that for the first time he felt nothing. He tried to understand it and it was like he always had something but didn't know it till it was gone. He realized that living in the kingdom and being around the king you have a happiness that was euphoric, like a high. The high was gone. He felt so plain. He felt like something died around him.

"Lucarious, Lucarious, are you all right?"

"Yeah, I'm ok."

Realizing that every pet in the original zoo was now dead, he realizes something else changed. Suddenly he was surrounded by little miniature beings.

"Who are these and where are my friends?" he wondered. He thought to himself, "Did they all die like these zoo creatures?" Then after looking into the face of the one who was standing in front of him rambling on and on and on, he realized this was Zansibar.

"Zansibar? Is that you?"

"Yes, why?"

"You look so different."

As soon as that came out of his mouth he too remembers the king handing everyone the mirror. He realized that he is no longer beautiful, nor is he tall. Suddenly, terror went through his body. He realized during the fall to the earth he lost his looks and his height. He was a little taller than Kana. Kana was 12 foot tall, one of the tallest citizens. He realized he was still the tallest out of all the rebellion. But he now was only a foot and a half tall. The entire rebellion was only a foot tall.

"What in the world happened to us?" is all he could make out.

"GIVE ME A MINUTE !!!!!!!!" Lucarious screamed at Zansibar. Zansibar was so surprised he started to walk backwards. He kept walking until he tripped and fell over on his backside. He stood up and still looking at Lucarious, he ran away. Lucarious sat down and tried to collect his thoughts. He sat there and collected himself until his breathing was a steady rate.

He thought to himself, "Well, I guess I need to go and gather everyone up. We will need to go and regroup."

"Zansibar! Zansibar, where are you?" He sees someone running towards him.

Chapter 11

"Lucarious, what is it?"

"I need you to go and find everyone, have them go to our cave, the one that we met in so many times before. Gather everyone up and we will figure out what our next plan of attack is."

Zansibar starts telling everyone to meet. They all walk around and tell each other where to meet. Lucarious heads straight to the cave. He enters the cave and the torches are already lit up illuminating the way. He thought it seemed a little strange but keeps on walking. He gets to the meeting room and the torches inside the meeting room are also all lit up. He walks over and notices there are mirrors placed on every wall. He walks over and suddenly, like a truck load of bricks falling on his lap, he realizes nothing is the same. He is frozen in time just standing and staring into the mirrors. He can't move. He no longer looks the same. He looks terrible and he is so short, he is so small he turns around and sees the table is too tall to reach. That's how he short he has become. The mirrors make him understand what happened.

"RAAPPHHHHH! RAAAAPPPPHHHHHH!! RAAAAPPPPHHHHH!!! YOU WILL PAY FOR THIS!!! DO YOU HEAR ME? I KNOW YOU HEAR ME! RRRAAAAAPPPPPHIIHHHH!!!!! YOU WILL PAY! I PROMISE YOU! YOU WILL PAY! AAAAAAAAAHHHHHHHH!"

He runs over and picks up a rock and starts to smash every mirror on every wall. He smashes and smashes them into tiny little pieces. They are all being crushed when the rebellion members start to walk down the long entranceway. They hear glass smashing and being busted up. They hear Lucarious yelling and growling and spewing hatred. They all look at each other and shake their heads. Zansibar walks in and stops Lucarious. "WOAH! WOAH! WOAH! Slow down! Stop! Stop! Stop it! Ok, ok, everything will be ok, stop! You need to sit down and rest. We all have to rest. We need to take some time to get a grip on what happened."

Lucarious actually listens for once. He hops up on the chair and sits and waits.

Booka walks into the room and says, "Lucarious, the earth no longer looks like it used to, the land that once was one big piece has broken away and fallen into many pieces. Our force of hitting the earth has changed everything."

Lucarious looks up at him and says, "Really? That's interesting." He thinks to himself, "We changed the earth. We changed the earth, it's not the same and we killed his precious zoo pets, things, ah whatever they are, we killed them. Interesting. They drowned to death, but we didn't. Interesting. Huh, well that's good to know, but where is the rest of the team?"

"That's just it, Lucarious, they are scattered all over the place. They're all located on a different piece of land. I already sent scouts to fly over to the other pieces of land to inform everyone there is a meeting at the old meeting place. They should be

Chapter 11

here in a few hours. It seems that the lands are very far apart and even if they fly faster than they have ever flown, it's going to take a long time to get here.

"Very nice, good job Booka, good job. I like what I hear. You are loyal and I like it."

"Thanks, Lucarious. But now we should rest till they come."

"Yes, Booka, rest, because we have a lot of work coming our way."

"Lucarious?"

"Yes, Booka?"

"Why are the table and chairs so tall? What happened?"

"Booka, grab a handful of team members and tell them to cut the legs off all the chairs and the tables to accommodate our new bodies."

A few days later the entire rebellion is there and accounted for. The leaders are sitting at the table. The rest are sitting in their chairs.

Lucarious begins to speak.

"Fellow team members..."

"AAAHHHHHHAAAA!" someone screamed.

He suddenly stops talking and looks up and says to the member who is screaming, "What is it? What's wrong with you?"

He points to the ceiling. He realizes that there is mirror he missed. The entire rebellion just got a glimpse of what they look like. They knew things were different but didn't realize what their faces looked like. Lucarious clenches his teeth together and starts to growl. His face turns red and he picks up the closest thing to him and throws it. The mirror shatters into a million pieces and then falls all over everyone. When the dust settles, they all look around and are all too afraid to move. So they just sit still—very, very still. Lucarious stands back up and he starts to pace back and forth as he is talking.

"As we all know, our attempt to overtake the throne was not successful. We didn't reach our goal. But we did reach a goal and that is what we must focus on. We did not fail, we succeeded. We no longer have to follow around that disgusting creature called Jira, we don't have to wipe his mouth and wipe his noise every time he sneezes. We won; we now are no longer his servants. We won!"

Every one cheers and is now back to a happy mood.

"But there is one thing. We cannot go back to the kingdom and try to overtake the throne. It doesn't seem possible yet. But I have an idea. If we can't hurt King Raaph physically we can hurt him emotionally. There is something that is here on the earth with us that is sooooo precious to him, something that he loves so much. So much so that he has to come and visit it every day. So if we can't hit the king, we can hit Jira and Tamum. That will be the same as sticking our finger in his eyes. Hahahahhaha it will hurt. It will hurt bad. HAHAHHAHhahahaha . We can get back at him. So now we need to go and find out how we can get them to mess up their lives. But listen, no matter what, no matter what—if you figure

Chapter 11

it out you must come back and tell me. You will not do it. I will reward you for finding out what we need, but I will be the one to talk them into it. This is too important. I can't have anyone messing it up. So I want to break up into teams. I want some to go and hide inside the tops of the trees. Some can hide behind rocks, others in tall grass. But somehow we need to find out how to make ourselves look like the animals. If we disguised ourselves as animals we will be able to walk around and spend time with them and they won't even know it. So you over there, I want you to kidnap a few different kinds of animals and bring them back here and see how we can hide or look like them or whatever. So now you all have your jobs. Let's all rest for three days. Relax; become clear minded, because this job is too important. I don't want to rush into this. We have all the time in the world to mess this up for the king." The members of the rebellion did as their leader said. They captured a couple different animals. They brought them back to study. Many others hid in trees and behind rocks. They spent each spend day and night studying their every move. Others spied on Jira and others on Tamum. They studied everything they did while they slept, while they ate, while the worked the garden. They also studied their walk with the king. They really wanted to ruin their time with the king. They hated that he showed up and spent so much time with them. He hated everything that the earthly children stood for. Everything fueled their fire. Everything made them, drove them to the extreme. Lucarious watches this. Lucarious turns around and walks over to where some of the team are gathered. Lucarious stops and watches. One of his members jumps on the back of a wolf. He leans down and says turn and the animal turns, he leans into it ears and says stop. The animal stops. He tells the wolf to speak and the wolf lets out a barking noise. Lucarious eyes begin to go wide. He suddenly realized what he wanted to do will work. The animals actually listen to him. They obey the commands they were given.

"Amazing, simply amazing!" he says. "Good job my friend, now keep working. Keep it up, you are doing great."

Lucarious turns and walks away. His mind is going a million miles an hour. Now if we could do that without being seen, that would be amazing.

Lucarious heads back to the rock that he turned into his throne. He found a rock that looks similar to a seat so he decided that it would be his throne. He liked the fact that it sat higher up than the ground so he could sit back and watch his army perform their daily duties. He would watch over all. He could see and so could his army. They could see him and they all knew he was watching their every move. They couldn't get away without working. Lucarious drove them hard. He knew that even though there was nothing else to do, he knew he wanted to rule the earth.

He thought to himself, "Since I can't rule the kingdom, Jira is in charge of the earth, and I am

Chapter 11

stuck down here on this planet, I might as well take it over. But I really need to find a way to do both. First I want to make everything on the planet bow on its knee. Hahaha, but most importantly, I must get back at Raaph for the vile and hateful things he did to me. Who does he think he is? I need to kill Jira and Tamum. Then I can rule and reign on the earth. Then everyone will bow to me. Well, wait a minute, if I don't kill them, I could also make them and their children bow to me. Yes, that's it. I need to get the entire family to worship me. That shouldn't be hard. I can drive them crazy and get them to hate each other. I can also get them to quit thinking about King Raaph and get them to focus on themselves and then I will have them bowing to me. Hahahaha, yes, that is what I need to do. Sounds perfect."Lucarious sat back in his seat and he watched every move. He demanded they bring him everything. He demand his army to make the throne more comfortable, then demanded that they drop all that they are doing and do what he wants that very second. Lucarious gets even more carried away with each day. Zansibar, Booka, and the rest of the leaders walk back and forth throughout the entire camp. It seems that no one is exempt from the pushing of hard work. They are promised that if they hurry and get the answers, then that is it. No longer will they have to work. They need to hurry and get this all figured out for Lucarious. Once they get it figured out, then they will be allowed to stop working forever and they too can be worshiped. They are reminded of this every second of every day. They have learned a lot. Each time they figure something out that is new, they stop and present it to Lucarious. He always tells them its good but it's not enough. The entire army is getting better at flying, hiding, and just plain sneaking around. They all have learned so much. They start to grumble among themselves.

"I can't believe that Lucarious is working us so hard."

"Yeah, why doesn't he get off his butt and help us out? You'd think that he would be working hard, too."

"The sooner we get this done the sooner we can all be done forever is what he keeps saying, so why isn't he helping?"

Lucarious has had enough; he can't stand their grumblings any longer. He yells "Stop! Get over here!" They line up. He begins to turn very, very angry.

"I am sick and tired of listening to you complain. Nothing I do is ever enough. If I hear one more complaint about ANYTHING, I promise you won't like the job that you get. I promise you won't like what will happen to you. Now go back to work."

They all are staring at him with a blank stare. The stare alone is enough to tell anyone they really don't care what you have to say. They continue to stare and not move, looking at him like we don't care—we are unhappy and it's all your fault. They just don't move. Lucarious starts to walk towards his seat. He stops and turns to sit down when he realizes that everyone is still standing there staring at him.

Chapter 11

He becomes enraged and screams, "Get working you ungrateful, brain dead dummies!" They continue to stare at him for what seems to be forever. But in reality is just an extra second. Then they all turn and walk back to where their designated work station is. The entire time they walk back they grumble out loud and to each other how much they hate everything and everyone.

"Nothing is ever enough. Nothing."

Lucarious just sits there and shakes his head. "They didn't even stop complaining. They are...aah, never mind." Pretty soon a group of his army starts to walk toward his throne. They bring a bear to Lucarious and they say watch this. Then as the bear is walking around on all four of its legs, one of the members jumps up really high in the air, using all of his weight and force and heads straight towards the bear's back. And *boom* he disappears. It seems as if he is gone forever. Then pop, out he comes through the bear's mouth. He lands on the ground and rolls a few times and stands up and says, "Well, what do you think?"

Lucarious stands straight up and says, "Can you do it again?"

He says, "Of course."

"Can you get it to do what you want"?

"Of course," he answers again.

Lucarious starts to smile a huge smile. He can't believe what he just saw.

The Chosen One

"If I didn't just see it, I wouldn't believe it." He sits down. "Ok, do it again and then make it do something."

"What do you want me to make it do, boss?"

"I don't know, something, anything, just hurry up."

So he jumps up high and heads straight for the back of the bear. And, poof, he is gone, the bear stops and doesn't move for a moment, then suddenly he turns his head and stares at Lucarious. He stands up on his back legs and keeps his eyes on Lucarious. He walks over to him. Lucarious couldn't be happier. He just can't believe that one of his team members found the secret he has been hoping for. The bear continues to walk close to him. He is still staring at him. The bear is not taking his eyes off of Lucarious. As soon as he is close to Lucarious, he begins to roar. He roars and roars and roars. He gets louder with each roar.

Lucarious says, "Ok, enough, that is good enough. You can stop."

The bear then puts his face into Lucarious' face and his eyes to his eyes.

Lucarious says, "Ok, you can stop now!"

The bear looks him in the eye and starts to growl. Lucarious is trying to back up into the stone where he is sitting. He gently says,

"Ok, ok, calm down, it will be ok. Please, you can stop at anytime."

The bear growls for a moment and then, pop, out of the mouth of the bear comes the army soldier. He lands behind Lucarious just above his head and

Chapter 11

rolls onto the rocks. The bear stops, shakes his head and looks at Lucarious. The bear realizes he has his hands around his head and is hugging him so the bear sticks out his super long tongue and starts to lick Lucarious' face.

Lucarious started to yell, "Get him off. Someone stop him, get him off now! I tell you get him off!"

The bear doesn't want to stop. All the soldiers that came to show off their new discovery are too busy rolling on the floor holding their bellies laughing at Lucarious and the bear kisses. Finally after their laughter slows down, then they get a hold of themselves and they push the bear off of their boss.

Lucarious now decides that with the new discovery, they can not only hide in trees, they can hide in plain sight inside the animals. So he has a bunch of his soldiers go and climb high up into trees so that they can be hidden.

"All I want you to do is listen and tell me what is going on. What are they talking about? I want to know everything."

So the spies go out and climb into every tree that they see. Some trees are big enough that there are a few spies in each tree. They listen and study Jira and his wife every day. The longer time goes on, the more brave they become. They even started to stay when King Raaph showed up and walked in the garden. They couldn't believe that the royal family didn't even notice them up in the trees. If they did know they were up there hiding, then they did a good job of ignoring them.

One day one of the soldiers comes running as fast as he can towards Lucarious.

"Lucarious! Lucarious!"

So Lucarious sits still and waits for the news. Finally the soldier reaches the throne and, completely out of breath, he stops and bends over, breathing very, very heavily.

Lucarious says to him, "What is it? What's wrong?" He continues to stay bent over, still trying as hard as he can to breathe. "Come on, come on, and let's have it. Hurry, I don't have all day."

"We are going to send some animals into the garden to see if Jira can tell that my soldiers are inside of them."

He is still breathing heavily and starts to stand back up. He hugh hugh hugh he can't hugh hugh. Still breathing heavily, it starts to slow down.

"What? What are you saying?"

"He can't, he won't be able to."

"Jira won't know you are there? We haven't even tried it yet. What makes you so sure that you are correct? How do you know so much?"

"Well it's like this. One of the soldiers was relieving the other from his duty and they didn't realize how close Jira was. They were so busy with switching places, they didn't hear them coming. As Jira and Tamum were walking towards the tree, one soldier jumped down out of the tree and the other was

Chapter 11

slipping on the branches. The leaves were shaking and then Jira and Tamum stopped and stared straight at the soldier. He froze he was so scared that he had been caught. Then Tamum pointed up to the leaves and said, 'What was that?' Jira said, 'Ah it must be a squirrel jumping around up there. Maybe they are making a nest for their home.' The soldier still stood still. He was so scared but Jira and Tamum walked right past him. There was no way they didn't see him. I mean he really fell out of the tree and was standing at the bottom of the tree and was in plain sight. So after Jira walked away, he stayed frozen and then waited. After a minute or two he ran back and then we sent out a few fast running soldiers. They ran out in front of Jira and Tamum as they walked through the garden. So we kept it up we ran and walked in front of them. We stopped and jumped up and down, we ran around them, we did everything and they didn't see us. We can't be seen by them."

"What? What are you saying? This is ridiculous."

"We are invisible."

"That's just nonsense. How could that be possible and for what reason would he have us become invisible?"

So Lucarious walks over towards the garden. He walks into the garden and takes a few soldiers with him. They watch and look around and see that it's almost time for Raaph to show up.

"Hurry up and send someone out." So they pick the fastest runner they have. He runs out and runs a few feet in front of Jira and Tamum as they walk. He runs a lap around them. This time as he runs in front of them, he stops and then he waves his hands and jumps up and down then makes funny faces at Jira and then runs back to where Lucarious is hiding.

"Wow," Lucarious says, "I can hardly believe it. It just doesn't make sense. Why would he do that?"

So they walk away and decide they need to go back to camp and regroup. They need to change their strategy. The plans they have are good but with this new found information they can create a fool proof plan that is even better than the current one they have.

"This is going to be a lot of fun," he says.

After months of training, Lucarious is sure they have gained enough knowledge about their new found enemy. He also decides that the time for them to move forward is now.

He lines up his army and tells them, "The time is now and you all have worked hard. From now on, our jobs will be easy and we won't have to struggle anymore. From here on out everything should be easy. You soon will be able to lie back and be worshiped. Each and every one of you will be worshipped. Each and every one will be able to get what you worked so hard for. Now we must go back to the cave tonight. We will meet up and devise a fool proof plan. We are so close to taking over. We will rule and reign together. Now go and take the rest of the day off. But before you do that, return the animals that we

Chapter 11

"borrowed." Return them to their homes and then meet up at sunset when it is just about to get dark."

Lucarious heads into the cave when it is dark out. Although he now knows he can't be seen, he still enjoys traveling at night. He arrives to find the entire team have already lit the torches and are already assembled inside the meeting hall. They are all there and accounted for. He takes the main seat at the table. His top level advisors are already sitting at the table. They have been talking strategies for their first move. The best way to do anything is to divide and conquer. That is the way to win, they have decided.

Lucarious then sits at the table. He listens to all they have discussed without him. He likes what they have to say. He decides that although they are close, they haven't made the perfect plan. He listens and listens and thinks to himself as he is listening.

"Ok, here is what I think. We need to pick an animal to enter into and then get them to talk to the animal. We need the animal to befriend them, follow them and find the perfect way to get them to mess this thing up."

One sitting in the crowd yells out, "How will you get them to mess this whole thing up?"

"I think the answer is to get them to doubt the king's words, convince them they are missing out and the king is holding things back. The rest will have to unfold one day at a time. We will have to see what happens. Does anyone have a quick and easy solution for this problem?"

One of the troops in the back yells, "I do."

Lucarious waves him up front. When he gets there Lucarious asks him, "So what information do you have for me?"

"Well, I know that there is a tree that they talk about. This tree is supposed to be the only one they can't eat from."

"Which tree is it?" Lucarious asks.

"Well, whatever it's about, it must be important, because Jira rolled two black rocks in front of it just to make sure that he didn't grab it by mistake and eat from it. That's all I know."

The soldier turns around and walks back to his seat. "So the king tells them they aren't allowed to eat from this tree. Ok, ok, ok...hum. Well we will have to see what is up with this tree."

Zansibar says to Lucarious, "I have a soldier who is the best of the best. He can go into a body and get it to do anything he wants it to. I have been watching them practice and he is the best. Would you like him to enter the body of the animal and do what you want him to do?"

"No, no, no, that won't be necessary."

"But Lucarious, he is the best of the best. I promise you that you won't be disappointed."

"Listen up, Zansibar this one is too important! I can't trust this one to anyone. It is so important that I need to do it myself."

No one can believe what Lucarious just said. He hasn't done a thing since the fall to the earth, as they

Chapter 11

call it. "I can't allow this to be messed up. I will do it, I am it."

So the next day Lucarious eyes up each animal as it walks around the garden. He watches each one for awhile. This goes on for days. He decides that the snake will be the best choice. The snake is small enough that it can crawl up a tree. It is fast moving and can hide well. So he decides to try it for himself. He jumps into the snake and crawls around the garden. After a few minutes of practicing, he comes out and says that wasn't so hard. It was pretty easy.

He sends for Zansibar. When Zansibar finally arrives, he tells him that he would like to talk to the soldier that Zansibar claims is the best. So Zansibar goes and finds him and presents him to Lucarious. Lucarious asks him to explain what he has learned and how he became the best of the best. The soldier unhappily divulges his secrets. He and the rest of the rebellion are realizing fast that things will never be the way they were promised. If they could mess up Jira's life and they could get King Raaph to leave and never come back would they really rule the earth? Would they really be worshipped? How long till Jira starts to have children and how many children will he have to have before someone bows down to him? So many unanswered questions.

After Lucarious takes all the information from his soldier, he then sends him back to the training grounds. He takes the knowledge he has learned and uses it against the animal. Lucarious waits till the morning and then sends for the snake. The rebellion captures the snake and brings it to Lucarious. He jumps into the body and walks into the garden. The garden is so different from the outer earth. Colors are brighter and the light doesn't hurt the eyes. Everything is different. The smells are overpowering coming from the flowers and all the living plants. You can't help but notice the smells. Then he slowly finds Jira and Tamum. Once he has found them, he slowly sneaks up on them. He hangs around them and listens to them and doesn't do much. At first he tries not to be noticed, then as time goes by, he allows them to know that he is hanging around.

Finally Tamum says to Jira, "Do you think it is strange that the snake is following us and hanging around the home we have?"

"No, before you were here they all took turns hanging around and even climbed in next to me as I slept. The animals loved to spend time here before you came. They must be becoming comfortable with you being around also. They probably will hang around more and more and more."

"Ok, Jira, if you say so. They just keep spending more time, then one day it's gone." Tamum says to herself, "Hey, I haven't seen that snake around. I wonder where it went. They decide it's time to go. After a hard mornings work, they decide to sit under a tree and eat lunch.

Chapter 11

Jira says "I'll go and get the food. Sit here and take a break." So Jira wonders off looking for the perfectly ripe food.

Tamum hears someone calling her. She looks up and says, "Hello, who's there?"

"Over here," she hears. So she stands up and starts to walk towards a tree. "Over here." Immediately she realizes that it isn't any voice she ever heard before. She says hello again, listening to see where the voice is coming from. "Over here, my dear."

She walks over to the tree and says, "Is this tree talking to me?"

The voice says, "Why, my dear, haven't you ever talked to a tree before?"

"Uh, no, no, I haven't talked to a tree before, nor did I think that a tree could talk."

The tree starts to laugh. The snake comes out from behind the leaves and says, "No, it's me, silly."

Then the snake pokes his head out of the leaves and starts to talk again.

"It's me, the snake, haven't you talked to me before?"

"No."

"Really? I thought you told me to go and I was hanging around too much?"

"Ok, I did say that, but I was thinking out loud, I wasn't talking to you."

"Well that is funny, it sure seemed like you were talking to me. But ok, then we won't talk."

"Oh, no," she says, "Please don't stop keep talking.

"You act like you never talked to any of the animals before."

"But I haven't, I never did before."

"Well maybe they just don't want to talk to you."

"Are you telling me that all the animals are able to talk?" Is that what you are trying to say to me?"

"Yep," he says, "But apparently they didn't want to talk to you. Are you sure that you are nice enough to them?" He then laughs.

"Yes, I'm nice."

"Ok, well I must go and you must eat so we will have to talk later." He climbs away very quickly and she stands there dumb founded, not sure of what to think about what just happened to her.

Moments later Jira comes back carrying a handful of good things to eat. Jira is talking about everything, not really taking any time to listen to his wife, let alone let her speak. This is where he first went wrong, not caring enough to allow her to talk at least half the time. So she smiles and pretends she is listening and thinks about what just happened to her. She tries to interject a few times but he is too excited about the day and the king's visit that he doesn't even notice that she is in her own little world. So she just keeps it to herself. The snake that is hiding can hear the entire thing and is extremely excited to know that he is being kept a secret. He is excited. The next few days as Jira jogs off looking for food, the snake comes back for its daily conversation. They end up talking about many things. It becomes such an everyday occurrence that

Chapter 11

she doesn't even realize how strange it is that she is talking to a snake, let alone any animal.

So one day, Jira finds the food very close to where she is waiting and accidentally sneaks up on her. He wasn't trying to spy on her; he just didn't go far and didn't make that many noises when he returned. Jira saw her talking to the tree but he also heard a different voice similar to his voice, nothing like his wife's voice. So he places the fruit down and gently walks up behind her and suddenly realizes that she is talking to a snake.

He says, "What in the world are you doing?" She jumps and lets out a scream. The snake goes immediately into the leaves so it can't be seen. He says to her, "What are you doing?"

"I'm doing what I do every day when you go to get the food. When you leave me here all by myself, I get bored so I talk to the snake."

"Talk to the snake? Talk to the snake? How ridiculous is that?"

"It's not. Besides, he says they can all talk."

"If they can talk, then how come I never heard them talk before? Well, well, how come?" he says.

She walks over to the sheep and tells it to move. It does.

"See, it listens to me, it understands. It just doesn't want to talk; it doesn't have anything to say. So don't tell me it doesn't understand what we are saying."

Jira stops and scratches his head and thinks about it and then realizes the animals always obey when he talks to them so they can understand what he is saying at the very least.

So he says, "Ok. Let's eat."

So they sit down and eat.

"But tomorrow I must talk to the snake." So this became the daily ritual. They talk to the snake while eating lunch and then finish working and then go and walk with the king in the afternoon.

So one day as they have spent hundreds of afternoons talking to the snake and being entertained by him and his wisdom, they become so close that the snake even climbs to the top of the tree and then finds them the juiciest fruit, the most ripe fruit on each tree and brings it to them.

This particular day they where working near the forbidden tree and the snake says, "Come on and let's get lunch." So he climbs up the forbidden tree and brings them down the shiniest and most juicy fruit they ever saw.

Jira says, "No, we can't."

The snake stops and says. "Why not?"

"King Raaph told us that we aren't allowed to eat from that tree."

"Oh, he did, did he?" says the snake. "Oh, it figures, that's just like him—holding back from everyone."

"What do you mean, holding back?" says Jira.

The snake comes close, looking around to make sure no one can hear him, and says, "Because if you eat from this one, you will become just like him. You will know good and evil. You will know more than

Chapter 11

anyone, more than me, and then you will be just like him. But that's ok. You don't want it. You don't need it. He said you shouldn't eat it. But if you don't want to be just like him, then ok. Ahh, never mind."

Jira looks and thinks about it and says, "No, come on, let's get food somewhere else."

The snake looks at Tamum and says, "What about you?"

"Jira says that King Raaph says we will die if we touch the tree, so of course I won't eat from it."

"Die? Die? Did you say you will die?"

"Yes, that is what we said."

The snake's eyes are beginning to grow huge. He just figured out the key to unfolding the very thing he wanted. "Die? Die. See, that's what I mean! You won't die if you touch it. Just look at me. I am all over the tree and I didn't die. But he doesn't want you to be near it at all, so you better not eat from it. We wouldn't want you to become just like him now would we?"

"I ...I...I don't...I just don't know."

"Touch it? I am touching it. Touch and see, you won't die."

Tamum looks at Jira, he nods and she touches the tree. She didn't die. Nothing happened, in fact, nothing at all. Her heart was racing very, very fast and nothing happened.

"See, I wouldn't lie to you, you didn't die when you touched it. See, I am just trying to help you."

"Ok, ok, ok, that's enough. We need to eat and get back to work."

Jira walks over and grabs her hand and gently pulls her aside and together they walk around and find lunch. They eat and talk about what they will get done before the king's arrival.

Tamum asks, "Jira, why didn't we die?"

"I don't know, but I do know that I was told before you came to live with me, not to eat from the forbidden tree."

"Well, why is it here if we can't eat from it?"

"I don't know that either. I really don't know. Guess it is a way of testing us."

"But what if the snake is right, what if King Raaph is holding back from us?"

"Well, Tamum, he hasn't taught us everything we need to know yet, so let's just expect when the time is right we will know all the answers to everything."

So for the next few days, Jira suggests they keep all talking to the snake to a minimum. This only drives Lucarious nuts. He can't wait much longer. The rebellion has already been overly anxious for a long, long time. He wants and needs to be worshiped. But then he comes to his senses and realizes that he better take his time and not rush it. This is his only chance that he can see with no other way around it that he can figure. One step at a time, one step at a time.

After making only small talk, they see the snake is still hanging around. They decide that it is ok to allow the snake to tag along. They openly welcome a

Chapter 11

different personality to talk to. The three of them talk and work the land day after day. They take care of the animals and the water and the land. Everything is growing and things seem beautiful. The snake seems to always appear at the right time. Lunch time and just before bed. Although they aren't noticing it, these are the two points in the day when they are tired. The snake has already noticed the more tired they are the more vulnerable they are. He realizes that they aren't willing to think or concern themselves with much; they are just plain worn out. So the snake decides to take advantage of this situation. He quietly runs through the garden early in the morning noticing everything he can that needs help or changes made to it. Then at lunch time while they are eating, he tells them and tries to push them harder and harder every day. How proud the king will be if they just work a little harder. Every day the snake helps shape their view of themselves. He takes away, in their minds, that they are loved for just being. They don't have to do anything to receive the love of their king. But the snake makes them think they need to work hard to be loved. He sees how he can shape and mold these two with just a little talking to. A little whisper in their ears goes a long, long way.

Time goes on, and day after day they work the garden, never taking a day off. There was no need to take a day off. Life seemed so perfect. Every day the king would bring his family for a visit and they would either play games or have a teaching and learning day. There was nothing but joy and happiness all over the place.

The king would remind them over and over again that the earth belonged to them and that they were to take control of it and everything in it. They were to tell everything what to do and how it should work and what it should be like. He was trying to hint around to them about them listening to the snake. He could also tell that they were getting more and more done.

Since they seemed more tired and over worked each day, he sat them down and told them a story.

He told them that a mother bird built a nest and laid many eggs.

"Not all the eggs hatched into baby birds, some just never hatched. But the ones that did, the mother loved and took care of with all that she had in her. She loved each one. Well, one grew a little bigger and told his littler brothers and sisters that they need to hurry and fly because mother would love them more if they acted like big birds instead of baby birds. He told them that they better hurry. They watched how much the mother interacted with the bigger brother and how he would try to steal all of her attention. So one day, they figured he must know what he is talking about, so they jumped out of the nest before they were ready."

"The mother was too busy looking for food. She wasn't anywhere to be found. Since they weren't ready, they hit the ground and broke some bones.

Chapter 11

They were in terrible pain. They laid there and cried and cried and cried and then when it was time for the mother to return she saw what happened and picked each one up one by one and took them to the nest. So after many, many attempts they finally admitted they wanted her to love them as much as she loved the bigger brother, so they thought they would learn how to fly so she had to love them then. She explained what love was and how she fed them and kept them warm and did everything because they weren't ready to do it for themselves. That is love, she said. So now since you have broken your bones you may never be able to soar in the sky and you may have to crawl in the earth and look for food that already hit the ground. Sure enough they did hurt themselves bad enough that they couldn't fly. They couldn't live as they were designed to live. So they had to rely on other birds knocking food down to the ground while they were eating. In other words they had to eat others' scraps and even rely on rotten food to eat after they got older. Never try to be loved, just be loved."

"You working yourself too hard isn't going to make me love you more. I can never love you any less. So just don't work yourself too much, don't strive, just be. When you listen to others and not the one who loves you, it will change the way you live your life forever."

The king smiled and hugged them and told them he loved them and they would see each other tomorrow.

Chapter 12

They talked about his story and figured he must know about them talking to the snake.

"He keeps bringing up about us taking control of things and the earth and, and, and. How do you think he knows Jira?" she asked.

Jira suddenly goes back inside of his head and remembers just before King Raaph introduced Tamum to him, he realized that the king was reading his mind. "Tamum, he read my mind. He read my mind the day that he introduced me to you. He read my mind. I was thinking instead of listening and he told me to calm down and pay attention. He knows, he knows. Tamum, oh, wow, ok, I didn't know that. I didn't even consider that. So he knows, ok, well then, he knows. But if he knows, then how come he keeps asking us what we did every day? Not sure, I'm just not sure. We can ask him tomorrow."

So after the next day the king and his family come as usual and they decide to ask him. They tell him it's their turn; they want to ask him questions. They want to pick what they get to learn about. So they ask him

Chapter 12

all kinds of questions, things that have been on their mind for a long time. They come to the day that Jira realized that he read his mind. So the king explains how he blocks some things so they can be a surprise.

"It wouldn't be fun for you or me if I knew what I was getting for a gift before I got it now, would it?"

Everything makes sense to them, so after many hours of asking questions, the king feels they are satisfied with all of his answers.

They both continue to live the life that was given to them and they continue to grow the garden into a beautiful place. Everything seems so perfect, so content. They both couldn't be happier. In fact they don't have any idea what it is like to not be happy. As they work their way around the garden they have the snake come around and talk to them a little here and a little there. The snake is realizing that everything he does or says is canceled out by their walk with the king. The more time they spend with the king, the less they are easily swayed. He realizes that he must stop the walk. Lying seems the only way is to get them to know about evil. The king won't be around evil. If he could just get them to go against the king and get them to have evil desires in their hearts, King Raaph will leave and never be able to come back.

They end up back at the forbidden tree as they always do. They make a circle around they garden when they are pruning the trees and checking the growth and making sure the leaves are doing well. They make sure the trees are getting enough water and that the sun isn't too hot for them. They check for homes of different birds and animals such as the squirrels. They make sure the nests are well made and are being maintained and to see if they can help in any way. When they get back to the forbidden tree, they usually just give it a glance from far away and kind of ignore it. So this particular hot day in the garden, the snake climbs back up into the forbidden tree and asked Jira and Tamum to come there.

"You know if you touch this tree you won't die." They both shake their head and say, "Yeah we know."

"So why do you ignore it? It's getting big and kind of needing repairs. So why don't you fix it? You can touch it; nothing will happen."

They step back and look. They have to agree that the tree is not quite as appealing as it once was. It's a little over grown here and there. So they figure it needs attention. They climb up on the rock and prune it. They cut here and there. They inspect it and climb all over it as if it were any regular tree.

Nothing was much different except the fruit. For some reason the fruit was extremely plump and tasty looking. It had a glow to it like none of the others did. It seems to call to you. Jira reached up and tugged on the fruit just a little bit and nothing happened. It seemed like it was stable. He climbed down. He looked around and said, "You know Tamum, how come there aren't any fallen fruit? There is none of this fruit on the ground rotting. This one doesn't seem like it wants to reproduce itself. I wonder why that is?"

Chapter 12

"Well, maybe since we aren't allowed to eat from it, there is no reason for it to reproduce itself."

So they finish the job. They look to the sky and see it's about that time.

Jira says, "Ok, let's break for lunch and we will come back and see what it looks like when we are done eating." So they walk over and grab some fruit from other trees. The snake again climbs its way up the forbidden tree. He calls to them to come and look, so they walk over expecting to see something they missed.

"Yes, what is it?"

"I just think that you have been here long enough, you work so hard and have been for so long and what do you get for all your work? Nothing. Don't you deserve something more than just a good job now and again? Don't you deserve much more than that? If anything you should give yourself a treat."

"What kind of treat?" Jira asks.

The snakes wraps is self around the forbidden fruit. "This will do. This will do just fine."

"Nah," he says, "We already ate, and we don't need that."

"Look, here is a small one. Look how delicious it looks. It could be desert. I saw the king bringing you pie from the kingdom. I bet the fruit they use is just like this. That's why he doesn't want you to eat, because then you will know his secrets. Then he can't pretend to have something great from the kingdom to bring to you. It's been here the entire time. There it is sitting in front of you. You could have had it every day, instead of once a month when the king feels like bringing it to you."

Tamum says, "You know, it does kind of look like that filling from inside the pie that we eat with the king. Maybe he is right; maybe we had the pie fruit here the whole time and didn't even know it. Maybe it doesn't have to be a special treat any more. Maybe we can cook it for the king and surprise him. What do you think, Jira?"

"I think you are right, it does look like it. It seems to be something that would taste great and it never falls to the ground and rot like the others, so I'm guessing that King Raaph made it not to fall because it was too valuable to. But I'm not sure. You remember the story about the bird?"

"Yes, Jira, why?"

"I can't stop thinking about that story and we both didn't like the way it turned out. Do you really think the king who loves us so much he can't stop telling us how much he loves us, would ever allow us to live like that? He said there were consequences for our actions."

"Yeah, but I think the snake is right, there is something going on with this fruit. There is something very special with this fruit. I want to taste and see what the king has hidden from us." She reaches up and tugs on it and it doesn't come off. She reaches up with both hands and pulls hard and pop, it falls

Chapter 12

off and into her hand. Jira's heart is pounding; he doesn't know what to do.

She says, "I can't take it any longer, I must see what he doesn't want us to know."

Jira feels like everything is in slow motion. He wants to scream, he wants run, he wants to knock the fruit out of her hand but he can't, he won't.

He just stands there and stares and says, "Don't do it."

She laughs. "Oh, Jira, come on, just one little bit and I'll tell you if it is the same as the pie. One little bite. I won't eat the whole thing."

"Ok, I guess if you must, but seriously just one tiny little bit, just a taste."

The snake can't believe his eyes. He is staring at them thinking to himself; this is just too easy.

She wipes it and then bites into it. The juices flow down her face and she chews away. She looks at Jira and says, "Mmmm, this is good. It's not the pie but it is so, so good." The juices that were on her face get enough to them they hit the ground and instantly kill the grass and turn it black. Jira jumps backwards. He can't believe it; he has never seen anything like this before. This can't be good.

Just after thinking it he says it to her. "This can't be good." He points to the ground.

She sees the black grass and says, "Uh oh." She finishes her mouth full and says, "That was great, and I'm not dead. See, the snake was right, I didn't die. King Raaph was holding back from us."

The Chosen One

Jira says. "It's too late. We messed up big time. There are going to be huge consequences. I can see it now."

"Stop, stop it! Just stop. We are fine. I am fine, just fine. Knock it off. I'm not dead and I'm not going to die, right snake?"

She looks up to see the snake is nowhere to be found. "Snake? Snake! Where are you snake? Jira, where did he go?"

"I don't know, but I really think you are in trouble."

"Oh, well then I am in trouble. I am. If I am in trouble for that, then I might as well finish it. It is super yummy. Here have a bite."

"No. No! I won't do it I won't eat it."

"Oh, come on."

"Stop.

"I told you."

"Tamum?"

"Yes, Jira?

"I think I better eat it, too. I think that if you die I don't want to be here alone. I lived without you and I can't bear the thought of living one minute without you. I can't do it again. Especially since I now know you. Before I knew you, I knew I was missing something but I didn't know what it was. Then I met you and I found out what that thing I was missing was. It was you, the whole entire time it was you. I can't be here without you. I won't."

So he too reaches up and pulls very hard and *pop* off comes the fruit. He, too, eats it up and the water

Chapter 12

and juice spill out of it, run down his face and kill anything that it touches. He looks over and she is done eating and she is giddy and laughing.

She is smiling from ear to ear. "See, I told you nothing would happen. I didn't die. See."

Then after he finishes he too, feels a little funny. He looks over at her and it seems that the fluffy stuff that follows the king around was falling off them. This was stuff that they really never noticed before. The king left a trail where he walked, but it was now disappearing from their bodies. He looks over and sees her entire body. He says, "You are naked. Look."

She looks down and for the first time she sees the middle part of her body. She looks over and it is lifting off of his body, too. They realize now they are in trouble. There is no way for them to hide this. Everyone will see that they are naked, just like the animals.

No way to hide, they look at each other and Jira says, "Run, Tamum, run to the thicket. Run. We will hide our bodies in there. No one will see us in there." They start to run towards it and both fall. They both are paralyzed and can't move one part of their body.

They can't move, but they can think. They close their eyes and start to cry as they realize they are in trouble. Then suddenly they both feel this numbness over take their bodies. All they hear is a *wap wap wap wap* inside their heads; then it's as if in their minds comes a movie. They close their eyes and they see a man sneaking up on another man. He picks up a rock and slams it into the other man's head. They see water falling from the sky and filling the earth. They see a big boat and thousands upon thousands drowning in the water. They see a tower and then see people all talking and they can't understand one, let alone the entire group speaking. They see people grouping up and all going their own way. They see two twins being born and see hate in each other's eyes. They see Islamic writing and Jewish writing written on either of their chests. They see both running in opposite directions they see wars and wars and wars coming from each of their seeds. They see women being beaten and abused, they see their bodies being mutilated and forced into dark rooms with men. They hear screams and screams of the innocent. They see Egyptians beating the seed of one of the twins; they see the seed running away to a far away land. They see wars after wars after wars. They see an army being built up and over taking the seed's new home. They see women cooking and eating their own children. They see a temple being built and being burned by the enemies. They see giants killing that same twin's seed. They see a young girl giving birth. They see the words redeemer written on his chest. They wish the wapping inside their ears would just stop and go away. They see the child being hunted and hunted and hunted. They see the child praying and seeing the sick walk and blind people seeing. They see him brutally beaten into a pulp. They see him hanging on a cross. They see

Chapter 12

King Raaph standing in the kingdom looking into earth and just pounding and pounding on this man hanging on a cross. They see Kadesha not being able to watch and then realize the man on the cross is the king's son, just an older version. They see Kadesha coming to the earth after her son's death and filling every friend of her son's with herself. They see an army being built with power and authority. They see miracles and people being blown away.

They see the face of the snake on a man. They realize this is the man who tormented the entire earth. They see many people filling what they could only guess to be the kingdom. They see many nations loving and praising the king's son. Then just as quickly turning their backs on him and begin spitting on him. They see huge boats crossing a large river. Boat after boat after boat. They see this new found land across the other side of the earth. They see people and the houses and the land and big buildings popping up all over the land. They see wars from across the river and then wars from the top of the land to the bottom of the land. They see a new style of government appear. They see that the bigger the new land gets, the less they bow to the king. They see big bright lights going up and lighting up the night. They see men giving money to women and taking them into a room and shutting the door. They see people buying bags of stuff from men in back alleys. They see them taking the stuff and injecting it into their arm. They see huge loud white things flying all over the sky and people climbing into them. They see them flying into tall buildings and then wars and wars and wars from this. They see war coming from the east across the river and the biggest whitest building that they ever saw being hit by a huge pointed thing.

They see destruction and more destruction and they see the white building burning to the ground. They see more of these pointed things hitting all over the land. People digging underground and people hiding in the houses and people killing each other for food. They see a new government come once again. They see the face of the snake and then he promises happiness. He helps everyone rebuild, he promises freedom and help to everyone. He feeds the hungry and makes the enemies shake hands. They don't get it, why the snake? They see him destroy everyone who doesn't bow and worship him as a King of Kings. Then *bam* they open their eyes and realize they are no longer paralyzed. The stand up and remember they are naked and run to the thicket.

Jira and Tamum can't even talk. They just sit there and shake. Then after a few minutes, Jira comes to his senses and then remembers how the king folded up big leaves to make cups and things that would carry. So he starts to bend and fold and twist together a bunch of big leaves making them coverings for themselves.

"Here take this and put it on. Now you won't be naked any longer." He starts on his clothing.

"Jira?"

Chapter 12

"Yeah, Tamum."
"What are we going to do? What did we do?"
"I don't know and I don't know. That's all I know is that I don't know what will happen to us. The king is going to see that we made clothes; he is going to ask us where that stuff went to. We will have to admit what we did."
"Do you think he will kill us? Is that what he meant we would die? Will he be so mad that he will kill us?"
"I don't think so."
"Why do you say that? How do you know he won't kill us?"
"Because Tamum, I love you and I could never kill you no matter what. No matter what. The king loves us with all that is in him. He won't kill us. We just need to ask him to forgive us and fix this terrible mistake."

The king realizes that it is time for his daily visit. He assembles the family and they start walking to the obsitorium. He tells them that things have changed, we are going to have a very different day on earth than what we are used to.

When they arrive, the king already has Nemola waiting at the obsitorium. They stand in the place they always do. King Raaph nods to Nemola and says its time. Nemola leaves immediately. The king and his family head toward earth. Nemola goes and tells his lead messenger to give out this message. He turns and goes immediately to the warriors and the messenger citizen's. Nemola heads to the palace. He turns on the projector. He heads over to the sound system and turns it on. The lights in the kingdom start to go dim. The citizens get confused as it is way too early for the lights to go out. What is going on? Suddenly through the sound system they hear their king. He is calling Jira's name. They all run for the palace, realizing the king's movie system was turned on. As they rush there, they wonder why the king did that. Did he leave it on from last night? Is it possible that he may have forgotten? They doubted that the king forgot anything, anytime, ever. So they all arrive and are talking among themselves. They realize it isn't a movie this time, it is real time. They are going to witness something as it happens. They are frozen with curiosity. Meanwhile Nemola's messengers have alerted the warriors and they are assembled at the obsitorium. When Nemola is sure they are all there and accounted for, they leave for earth.

"Jira? Jira, where are you?"

Kadesha says, "That's not like him. Most of the time, he is standing here waiting for us with the largest smile he could possibly give. Raaph, where are they?"

Raaph continues on, calling for him; in his head he doesn't want to be mean to his wife and not answer but doesn't want her to fully understand what is about to happen. So he gently leans over and says it's begun. Kadesha freezes. She is saddened and sick to her stomach. She can hardly believe that the rebellion has completely changed and influenced itself on the earth.

Chapter 12

"Jira, Jira where are you? Are you going to make me look for you? Are you hiding from me? Where are you?"

Jira and his wife are scared and have no idea what to do. They are hoping the king will just go away. If they take off the clothes they made they will be naked in front of the entire earth. If they walk out with the clothes they made everyone will know what they have done.

"What should we do? What should we do?" she keeps asking him.

"You know he's not going to give up that fast. Let's go."

So they both stand up and stand behind the bushes. Luckily the bushes are tall enough that only their heads can be seen. "King Raaph, here we are, we are over here."

"Oh, there you are. What are you doing hiding from us? Is this some kind of new game you were playing?"

"Uh, yeah, a game, yeah, uh, that's it, a game."

"Ok, silly now come out here. We need to eat some dinner together. It's time to feast."

Jira and Tamum just stand there not moving, frozen. They don't know what to do or what to say.

"Jira come on, get out of those bushes and get over here. We are all hungry."

Jira and Tamum are still frozen, not knowing what to do. So the king starts to walk toward them.

"What's wrong, what's gotten into you two?"

"Well, uh, you see. We are naked and don't want to be naked in front of you."

"Naked? That's silly. Who told you you were naked. You're not naked, come on."

Then suddenly the king stops and says, "Please tell me you didn't eat of the tree of which I commanded you not to. Please tell me you are joking and that you don't have the knowledge of good and evil, that you are both still innocent and only know good."

"Well, king, you see it's like this. She gave me the fruit and I ate it because she gave it to me."

"Jira? Jira, I can't believe you are blaming this on me. King don't believe him, it's not my fault, don't believe him. It's not my fault; it was the snake's fault. He tricked me into eating it. I didn't know what I was doing, he tricked me. Please don't be mad at me. Please don't be mad. Please let us go back. Take us back. You are our king, you created us and you can put us back. Allow us to start over. Please king, please."

"Oh no oh no...no no no no no no...what have you done? You have no idea what you have brought upon yourselves. You have no idea what you brought on your children. Nor do you have any idea what you brought on this earth. Why, why did you choose this path?"

Placing his face into his hands, he walks in circles. "It was the only path that you were not supposed to choose."

He removes his hands and for the first time all creation sees tears, tears for the first time. No one

Chapter 12

knows quite what to do because of his tears, no one ever experienced sadness. They stand there frozen and although they look emotionless, they are all being flooded with emotions, things they have never experienced.

"I would have given you anything; anything that you would have asked for could have been yours. Why? Why did you not listen? Why did you disobey? The devastation that will follow, well you will see, you will understand even more soon enough. No use dwelling on it now, it wasn't supposed to be this way. Things are always going to be harder. Well, son, I wish you hadn't chosen this path. But you did. Now everything will be harder for you. The work that you do will be a thousand times harder and instead of a few days to reap your harvest you will have to wait months. Haaaaa.."

He sighs, "...there will be thorns and weeds that will now plague you. It wouldn't be like it used to. You will see. You will work harder and sweat a lot. Things will never come as easy as they did. You will also lose some of your brain power. Right now you use all of your brain. Because of this I was able to teach you all that there is to know. Your children will only be allowed to use ten percent of what you currently have. They will not be able to retain everything the first time they hear it. They will struggle to learn things. They will have to attempt things may times till it becomes easier for them. They cannot have the knowledge that you have. Most of what I have taught and told you will die with you. It will be many years before they will discover things that you already know. They will need to learn how to build tools to see and know what you already know. Your body will wear out and not last forever. Daughter, oh my beautiful, beautiful daughter, oh, how my son loves you. I am not surprised that you could be deceived. Because I gave the instructions before you were brought here. You were not there when I told him what to eat and what not to eat. He should have taught you everything I taught him. I thought I gave you warning. I thought that you would take my warning and understand it. Should I have been more plain with my words?"

She immediately goes into remembering when she was walking around the garden and King Raaph had said to them, "I love you and you are my children. I bless you with all that is mine. It is now yours, also. I want you to prosper in everything you do. I also want you to have children; first, so you can experience these feelings that I have and also because I want more children. I want you two to be the beginning of the entire earth filled with my children. I will know everyone of them and they will all know me just as you two do. I will teach them how to love and honor each other. This is my plan. So go now and take over the earth, I give it to you so that you may rule over it all. You are the ruler of the animals. You are the ruler of the plants. You are the ruler of the birds of the air. Go and take control. I will worry about

Chapter 12

keeping everything else in perfect alignment. It will be me who provides the sun and the moon. It's my job to provide a balance of exactly what the earth needs. I will keep it exactly where it needs to be. I will control the weather. I will tell it when we will be in a cooling period or warming season, for I am the one who knows what the earth needs. No one else can control or change it. Those things will be up to me and no one else. Everything is going to be great. So go and always remember you are in control. Don't allow anyone or anything to take it from you."

"Daughter, daughter, are you listening to me?"

"What? Oh sorry no, I missed what you said. What did you say?"

"I was saying that I understood that you could be deceived. What surprised me is how much my son loves you. That he wasn't willing to live without you. So much that after you were deceived, he willfully sinned against me. That, my child, I did not see coming. By that, I truly am surprised. You, you my child were deceived, but not him. He didn't even try to stop you, he did not warn you, I created you to be each other's help mate, and you two were to complete each other. To make each other whole. You mean more to him than I guessed. Probably more than what I may have ever realized. Uuuuhhhh," he signs a long sign.

"Well, since you disobeyed me, there will be consequences for your actions also. I wanted the child birthing to go so easy for you, I wanted it to be full of love and joy and happiness. Because of your actions, it now has to be very painful to you. It will not be as enjoyable as I wished it to be for you. I wanted so much for you two, so many things. There is something else that will happen, and it is completely against everything inside of me...against my intentions and my desires. Man will always try to rule over women. My original plan was for you two to rule the earth together. You both were made in my image, with my life force, fluids and even my life cells. I made you and I was pleased with the both of you, you were my best creations I made. It will happen gradually, not all at once. Man will realize that he is stronger and will decide to dominate you. That is what will happen because of your actions. You listened to the lies of the enemy. The one who deceived you is the father of lies. He sure is good at it. Well, I need to deal with him next."

As King Raaph takes his eyes off his daughter, he remembers every one...all of creation is looking, staring at him, not moving, standing very, very still. Only their eyes dare to move. Following King Raaph's every step, every move, and every word. He looks at the warriors, the messengers, all the earthly animals, his children, and the creatures that surround the throne. Lastly, every fallen one is there, too. Every being frozen, fearful of even accidentally making a movement that might disrupt what the king is about to do next. King Raaph stops and begins to look around. He has the attention of the entire

Chapter 12

earth. Every creature everywhere is motionless. He continues to look. Then he stops and sighs. The look in his eyes is total sadness. No one has ever seen this, let alone experienced it. The most strange part, is that it is coming from the king who is always happy. He locks his eyes on the lamb. In a loud authoritative voice he says, "Lamb, come here." The lamb walks forward. He is completely willing to obey the one who created him, the one who loves him. He picks up the lamb and he starts to walk around in front of the entire earthly assembly. He walks back and forth stroking its wool. He announces and professes his love for this wonderful lamb. He talks about how the lamb in color is pure white. No dirt and no blemishes can be found on this lamb. He talks about how purity can be compared to the pure white clean wool of the lamb. He talks to them about how sin looks ugly. He explains to all that sin cannot be around him or that it would die. Everyone looks at Jira and Tamum. They seem to be getting weaker by the minute. Then they turn their eyes to Lucarious and his army. They, too, are getting weaker by the moment. He explains that he must hurry because his purity will dominate and kill any form of sin in its existence. He must keep moving on. So then he explains the innocence of the lamb.

"This little lamb did nothing wrong. It was perfect it all its ways. It did what it was created to do."

Now King Raaph explains that he is going to allow Jira and Tamum to come and live in the kingdom forever. There is great cheering that erupts from the messenger and warrior citizens. Jira and Tamum smile. They think to themselves that's it. This is almost over. A little while longer and they will all live in the kingdom and life will be perfect. Jira and Tamum step forward.

"Since you have introduced sin into this world you must die. The penalty for sinning is death. It is not fun or easy, it will be painful in most cases. That was your choice, not mine. No one who ever sins will be allowed to enter my kingdom. Ever. Since you and I both want you to come and live with me in my kingdom we must make a way. The only way is for someone who never sinned to take your place. Your sin must be placed on something that never sinned. This is what I am going to require. This way, there will be a way made for you two to enter my kingdom. So now how do we place your sin on someone who was innocent? Well, we must take the life of an innocent one and kill him. I love all my animals with all my heart. They all mean so much to me that I would do anything for them. But there is something greater in my kingdom than these animals. These animals are not as important to me as you are, my children. Since I have told you to take control of the earth and everything in it, I dare not break those rules either. So when I take the life, I will also teach you how to use every part of this body. We will make clothes for you two with the skin of this animal. Then we will make

Chapter 12

it a sacrifice. We will sacrifice this perfect blameless animal for your horrible, ugly sin."

He raises up the lamb in front of everybody. He grabs it by the neck and *cracccckkkkk*...he breaks it neck.

Everybody flinches and holds their breath, not knowing what to say or do. Everyone knew that the dinosaurs died on their own; they didn't live forever. Their life had a different purpose which wouldn't come for many years. Other than that, there was no death, there was definitely no murder, and there was no killing of any kind. This was also new and all so unexpected. King Raaph walks over to a huge gray rock with a flat top. He lays the little lifeless body on the rock. He walks over to where there are other rocks. He picks up a few until he finds the one he is looking for. He takes the rock and holds it up to the sun. He sees that it has an edge on it already. He walks over to the lifeless lamb and takes the rock and start to scrape it along the side of the other one. He does this for what seems like an eternity. Then he touches the outer edge of the small rock. He walks over to the lamb and starts to cut the lambs neck. He takes one of the cups of clay that he taught Jira to make and drains the blood from the body. He places the cup off to the side. He then cuts the skin off of it. He strips the muscles away from the outer skin. He walks the skin over to the stream and rinses it off. He brings it back and lays it back on the rock for the sun to bake the inner skin. He then picks up a few rocks and makes them into a pile. He then grabs some branches off of a few trees and then lights a fire. Once the fire is going, he pours the blood out of the cup and all over the rocks. He then picks up the lamb and burns the body.

King Raaph says in a loud voice, "I place your sins on this altar. The blood covers your sins." He says, "This body will burn so that you don't have to burn. This innocent lamb's skin will cover your nakedness."

He walks over to the trees and finds a rock. He carries the rock over and starts to hit the inside of the skin. Between his pounding and the sun baking, the inner part of the wool skin is hardening. He takes the sharp rock. He walks over to the stream and cleans the blood off of it. He then goes over to the wool and starts to cut it and shape it. He then walks over to Jira and Tamum. He tells everyone to turn away. Immediately everyone turns their back to Jira and Tamum.

"Remove those leaves from your body."

They both strip down. He places the clothing on their body, with the soft wool part on their skin. He smiles at them and asks them how it feels. They both say that they like the feel of it.

"Ok, you may now turn back around."

"I must hurry before they get any weaker," he thinks to himself.

"Lucarious you think you won, but you didn't. Do you see her? Do you? She will always be opposed

Chapter 12

to the snake. Her entire race will hate, despise and fear the snake. It will be so feared that it will become hunted and killed often. The snake will lose every leg that it has. It will have to learn to move using its belly. Without me teaching it. Its belly will always hurt, causing it to be in a bad mood all the time. This will make it easy for it to strike out all the time. The snake will become the lowest creature of all; even the cattle will try to stomp on its head. The horses will hate it. They will crush it. But that, that is nothing compared to what her offspring will do to you. There will be one who comes from her and he will crush your head and he will be victorious over you. He will hurt you and there will be no healing come to you. You will walk around in pain for longer than you can believe. This pain will never leave you. Through history you will have this pain walking around in misery because he crushed you. After that you and all the fallen citizens, all the creatures that eat from your table of lies will be tossed in a place of torment. A never ending torment.

"Zansibar step forward." Zansibar steps forward. "You are no longer called Zansibar but now and forever your name will be Horent. I will turn you into a place of utter and pure torment. Your body will now become this place that I am speaking of. All the other kingdom citizens that followed your command will reside inside of you. For your body will be Horent, it will be made for all of you that tried to set his place higher than me. Get ready to be extremely uncomfortable for a very, very long time. They will live inside of you. You will lie on the ground frozen in time. If they can't stand the heat living inside your body, how will you feel? The unfortunate part for me is that some of my children will make a choice to join you forever. I can tell you the sentence is living in pain and torment forever. Yes, some will come to live with you. There will come a time when I decide enough is enough. I will call that day judgment day. All will be judged on that day."

Lucarious interrupts the king. "So you will be judging your so called children on that day also."

"Listen here. You and your defiled kingdom and friends will be judged on that day for all the horrendous things you have done. But my children have nothing to worry about because judgment day for them is a celebration day. They will be judged in celebration of all the great and wonderful things they did. It is not a day to be feared but a day to have anticipation for. But I tell you today as sure as I stand here, there will come a deliverer. He will set the captives free, free from your clutches. He will give my children power over all of you and your vile putrid kingdom. This deliverer will come from my daughter and he will be victorious. Just wait and see. Although you and the world will always think that you have outnumbered me and my followers, I promise you, I will have more of my children living with me than you will have being tormented with

Chapter 12

you. Now flee from me, every one of you. You will always be known as the father of lies."

"Go now...go, you must leave."

But we don't wanna leave, we wanna stay."

Hot wet tears stream from both of their faces.

"Go."

"We don't want to."

"Go, you must go...go now. You must go..."

"But we don't want to..."

"You have to leave and never come back. Please don't try to come back." King Raaph is gently pushing, them prodding them to leave.

"Please, we don't want to King Raaph, please let us stay. Things will be different this time."

But they don't feel him anymore. They start to feel cold; they notice the clamminess of their own skin. They feel their skin on their body. There are so many things they never noticed before. Not only are they upset, they are in sensory over load. So many new things are happening all at once.

"Why can't we staaaayyyyy...why are you making us leave. This is our home you gave it to us. You told us to rule and reign over it and to keep it the way we want to. You told us you wouldn't have a say in the way we make it look. This is our place, don't make us leave; don't make us leave our own house. Where are we going to sleep or eat, where will we find food? How will we stay alive? King ? King? King?"

They turn around and it all looks the same. They can't tell which way they came from, it is all the same. Behind the force field barrier that is hiding the garden is King Raaph. He is staring and watching them walk away in confusion and disbelief. He, too, is feeling hot wet tears running down his face. For the first time on earth there are tears shed over this terrible mistake.

"They don't understand. They just don't understand. I will have to teach them, teach them many things. There is a lot to be done."

He watches as they wonder away, crying as they walk farther away. The garden is never to be found again.

"Kana, place a guardian in front of the entrance in case someone finds this place. No one can ever enter it again. Never."